DI

D0425223

The Virtuous Vixen

Other Books by Janet Templeton

LOVE IS A SCANDAL
LADY FORTUNE
THE SCAPEGRACE
LOVER'S KNOT

The Virtuous Vixen

JANET TEMPLETON

DOUBLEDAY & COMPANY, INC.
GARDEN CITY, NEW YORK
1985

All of the characters in this book
are fictitious, and any resemblance
to actual persons, living or dead,
is purely coincidental.

Library of Congress Cataloging in Publication Data

Templeton, Janet, 1926–
The virtuous vixen.

I. Title.
PS3558.E78V5   1985   813'.54
ISBN 0-385-19701-2
First Edition

Library of Congress Catalog Card Number 84-25902
Copyright © 1985 by Morris Hershman
All Rights Reserved
Printed in the United States of America

For
Julie Ellis
. . . and about time!

Contents

The Virtuous Vixen

CHAPTER ONE

A Peer for a Client

"I cannot think of any good reason for meeting yet another peer," said Heather.

"But why not?" Mrs. Shaw was annoyed.

"Because a man such as you describe, Mother, is not likely to be interested in a girl like myself."

"I fail to see any reason for pessimism," Mrs. Shaw said, tossing her head so violently that Heather suspected it might come off at its moorings. "Certainly you are a comely young woman."

That was true enough. Heather confirmed the knowledge once more by looking briefly at herself in what she always referred to as the hump mirror, an item which disfigured the northeast corner of the small sitting room at the home in Brook Street. Her bright red hair was done perfectly, parted in the middle just as Queen Victoria favored for young ladies. The royal blue silk dress, crossed with satin checkers, was enough to bring up the fine sky-blue coloring of her eyes. When she moved, the black velvet side trimmings intermingled with black chenille would stir, it was always hoped, sinuously.

"This young man, this visitor—"

"A peer," Mrs. Shaw put in determinedly.

"Granted, Mother, a peer. He will smile and speak with courtesy, yes. But as soon as I have answered, and he hears me, the light will go out of his eyes. From that moment he will bring his intellect, such as that may be, to bear only upon the matter which has brought him to the family threshold."

The same point had been raised in varying guises over many occasions during the last twenty-four months. Delphine Shaw, countering her daughter's attitude, always found herself reminding dear Heather about one development which was entirely factual.

"You are now a resident of some means and in the greatest city in the world," she pointed out again, as if for the first time. "For exactly two years, since February of '55, you, like Maurice and myself, have been flourishing in these competitive environs."

"That doesn't seem to make the least difference."

It was unnecessary to remind Mother in turn that London Fashionables of any age or either sex referred to the family's native town of Hawick as "Hoyk!" followed by a smile or sneer. Probably the word was an insult in general use among wealthier natives of The City, as London modestly styled itself. None could deny that a young woman who hailed from a community in Roxburghshire only half a day's ride from Edinburgh was no born-and-bred Londoner. To them, her place of birth constituted an unforgivable offense. Not until the family settled in the heart of civilization would seventeen-year-old Heather have believed that such an attitude could even exist, let alone prevail.

"You can understand," Heather remarked as her mother showed no inclination to budge from her aerie close to the doorknob, "why there seems no point to my meeting with this visitor."

"The Marquis of Thetford," said Mrs. Shaw, speaking as if the possessor of the title had descended from Olympus to mingle with mortals, "is very different from the run of peers."

Presumably this referred to the young man's financial condition. If he hadn't been possessed of the needful, he wouldn't be coming to Brook Street and the family home at this time in the morning, as Heather knew perfectly well.

"Thetford has just inherited a seat in the Lords because of the passing-on of his father," Delphine Shaw said. For her, it seemed, death was only a factor in improved conditions. "He hails from Norfolk."

This last was a piece of intelligence of which Heather hadn't previously been aware. An outlander himself, the Marquis might not identify her accent as Scots and be attracted before he knew or cared about the difference. She might find herself interested in him as well. It all seemed unlikely, but not impossible. Heather didn't consider herself infected by Mother's continually hopeful outlook, but some aspects of Mrs. Shaw's philosophy were bound to have seeped into her mind.

"In only a few minutes you will meet him," Mrs. Shaw promised. "You need not spend a moment longer with him than you wish."

The small sitting room door was opened enticingly, but not before Heather had signified her agreement. She would therefore refrain from going back to her room and sitting restively until dinner was served a little past noon.

There was the sound of footsteps in the upper hall, Maurice suddenly appeared in front of the small door. He turned to look in, then paused.

"Are you hoping to entrap the Marquis?" her brother asked.

Maurice Shaw was a short young man, with the family eyes, and light brows from his mother's side. His attempts at a self-portrait, with the aid of mirrors and daylight, had come to nothing, very largely because of his inability to paint those brows. In reproducing the images of others, however, he was far more successful. He was currently the most sought-after portraitist in The City, and had become so soon after Mrs. Shaw had brought the three of them to live here. Financial resources had promptly given out, so it seemed likely, as his gambling friends said among themselves, that success had been forced upon him as an alternative to destitution.

"There is no need to speak in such an appalling manner," Mrs. Shaw insisted, "about entrapment."

"Such a truthful one, you mean," he smiled cynically. One of his illusions was that the conversation he made was a lance that punctured all pretense and sham.

Heather had often enough overheard this type of familial sparring, but her mood now lacked the usual tolerant amusement.

"Will this man truly be here soon?"

"That is my understanding," Maurice said firmly. A look past the railing and down to the hall showed the Chinese bronze-columned clock. "Within moments."

"I will join you downstairs to greet him," Heather decided. "In that arrangement I can be quickly introduced and then take my leave if that seems indicated."

Maurice raised the brows that had proved so troublesome once when he was practicing his vocation.

"Has my speculation been wrong? Don't you have any plans to make of this wealthy peer a slave who grovels at your every wish?"

Mrs. Shaw chose to answer, and of course to do it evasively. "Your sister is not in the best of spirits at this time, Maurice."

"I see." He had occasionally received Heather's confidences in the matter of her Scottish origin and how it affected otherwise agreeable males in search of suitable and socially acceptable mates. He had remarked in turn that a Scottish upbringing was no more injurious to him in society than Moot Hill was to the south end of the community of Hawick. The lack of height, in his case, did prove troublesome. It was no time to try, however indirectly, to stiffen his sister's resolve, not in the company of a mother whose exhortations often caused wry amusement rather than reform. "Well, then, shall we proceed?"

Maurice led the way down the semicircular carpeted staircase. Some of the treads groaned in disregard of his light weight and Heather's. Mrs. Shaw followed at a distance, having decided to oversee her daughter's behavior and make critical observations afterward if that should prove necessary. She felt certain, though, that it wouldn't.

The circular hall, to which they descended, was bare of paintings for the reason that Maurice was unable to abide their use for mere decoration in his home. Despite an oft-proven gift for harmonizing colors, however, his sensible recommendations hadn't been heeded in decorating that area which led to the attic and his studio.

This area was done in what Mrs. Shaw felt convinced was the Chinese fashion. Wall panels were painted with dark lacquer, and hollow painted porcelain bases held several lamps, the bronze-columned clock, and statues of affable Orientals. Mrs. Shaw had been deaf to all complaints, no matter how august the source, insisting that the scheme she had employed was the best that could be devised. In spite of all evidence to the contrary in her own family, she considered it to be restful.

A series of knocks sounded upon the door in rapid succession.

"Less than a minute late," Maurice said with a look at his pocket watch this time, the gold hands gleaming in their gold case.

The maid had already opened their door and was admitting the visitor. Heather's first glimpse showed the stranger freeing the buttons of his single-breasted loose-hanging woolen coat, those buttons discreetly hidden by an underflap. The coat was taken from him and he stood in the hall looking uncertainly at the first of the household members who had come to offer greetings.

"I am Maurice Shaw, as Your Lordship may recall," the artist said, respectfully nodding. "It is good that you were able to come."

"I told you that I would be here."

The voice of Her Majesty's Right Trusty and Entirely Beloved Cousin, as a man of his rank was royally known, happened to be strong in timbre. The accent was not of London origin, confirming Heather's information. She pressed forward to gain a closer look at this phenomenon.

Julian Wyse, the Marquis of Thetford, was a dark-haired handsome young man in a dark-haired handsome jacket over a bright yellow waistcoat and a collar turned down stylishly over most of a large and spotted bow tie. His check-pattern trousers were worn with the correct looseness. This fashionable wardrobe appeared to make him uncomfortable. Calmness overtook the young peer once he had established contact and not been derided for wearing these clothes.

Maurice said, "I plan only to do some rough sketching today and I shan't keep you long."

"Whatever is suitable," the peer said, speaking with the calmness of resignation. "My family will be satisfied by the results, I feel certain."

He didn't have to add that only an obligation along those lines would make him consent to have a portrait painted at all, let alone a reproduction of himself in the costume that seemed to have been forced upon him. A belated awareness of the insult he had inadvertently given caused the Marquis to flush, darkening his complexion even further. Words of apology didn't come to him, let alone a lightly humorous observation that would have ingratiated him with this stranger and his cohorts. The Marquis looked away.

Maurice, absorbed by thoughts of the work to be done, had been unaware of any *faux pas*.

"Shall we," he began, gesturing to the carpeted semicircular staircase.

Only when he turned to lead the way did he realize that his sister impeded direct access to the route that would take both men up to his studio.

"Oh yes," Maurice said, almost gracelessly for once. "This is my sister."

"Your most obedient," the Marquis began, with a bow.

"Your Lordship," Heather said, acknowledging him.

The two words, as spoken with a strong tincture of Scots, galvanized the Marquis. It seemed that never before had he contemplated the notion of a comely female residing in London who had not been raised there, with ancestors who had imported the first horse into The City or at least put up the Regent Quadrangle in Piccadilly. Like himself, she wouldn't be taken aback by mannerisms that weren't, so to speak, the custom of the country.

"Your most obedient," he said once more, but in a different and far less mechanical tone.

Heather found herself looking warmly at the Marquis for the first time. In this slightly more detailed examination she became aware of the deep brown eyes with their irises that were almost as dark as the pupils. It was as if the eyes probed her, as if they were exceptionally alert to her responses. Certainly he was interested in her. On Heather's part it seemed pointless not to know more about a man whose social awkwardness was allied to a keen intelligence.

"You certainly do not hail from London." A smile transformed his face.

"Like my brother, I am Scots."

"I have not traveled as much as I would have liked, and a Scottish voyage, until moments ago, would have been of great interest. Now I feel that the best of what I might see there has already been transported to London."

"I hope I can believe that Your Lordship isn't being too kind."

She was aware of some disturbance in the background, and only then realized that her mother had belatedly descended the final step of the staircase.

Maurice said, "My mother."

"Your most obedient servant, ma'am," the Marquis said hesitantly. Upon being rewarded with a smile he let out a relieved breath and added, "Your family must be a source of great pride, Mrs. Shaw, I feel certain."

"I don't complain," said Delphine Shaw, calmly offering a prodigious understatement. "And I can assure Your Lordship that you are in excellent hands for a painting. My son is the most highly esteemed practitioner of that craft in all of London and for the best of reasons, as you shall see for yourself."

"I look forward to doing so," the Marquis said a little absently, his glance having returned to the painter's sister.

Heather blushed, and for the first time since childhood found herself wondering what to do with her hands.

As for Maurice, he had been made impatient by conversation when there was work to be done. Swiftly he took advantage of the Marquis' recent rejoinder to Mrs. Shaw.

"In which case, Your Lordship, let us get to the business of the morning, with your permission."

Julian, as Heather would always think of him from now on, was smiling at her.

"My studio is upstairs," Maurice said, raising his voice to accommodate the prejudices of a peer who was unable to focus his attention on the only activity that gave life its savor. "I paint and sketch up there, Your Lordship, the light being most suitable for my purpose, as you may imagine."

"To be sure," said His Lordship, speaking more loudly than the sentiment justified.

Maurice started up at last, then looked back to make certain he was being followed. In this he was disappointed. The Marquis had reached for Heather's hand and was holding it tenderly.

"We shall meet again," said he, in what was supposed to be a confidential whisper.

"Certainly we shall," Heather agreed, her heart pounding more swiftly.

Maurice coughed. "If I may trouble Your Lordship to follow me," he began.

Julian released her hand, although with a gratifying slowness in Heather's view, then turned to join the artist on the way up to the studio in the attic. He walked slowly. At the first opportunity he looked back at Heather and saw her smiling encouragingly up at him.

Mother waited until the males were out of earshot. A smile accented her resemblance to the daughter, taking away lines and clearly showing the woman as she must have appeared twenty summers ago.

"A pleasant morning and even a fruitful one for you—eh, my dear?"

Heather didn't want to think in terms of romance after having only met the young peer. On the other hand, she felt no inclination whatever to make some amusing remark at the expense of her mother's hopeful attitude.

"I presume that you will wait," Mrs. Shaw said, her eyes glinting, "until the session with Maurice has been completed."

"I shall be in my room." It was more sensible than prowling the lower floor and glaring at the clock.

"Keep the door open," Mrs. Shaw advised sensibly, tempering optimism with reality, "and refrain from making noise."

"I shall be sketching," Heather said. Like her brother, she wanted to commit an impression of the Marquis of Thetford to paper, although not for the same reasons. She particularly wanted to capture those strong quizzing eyes. She would be depending entirely on memory, but a vivid memory indeed.

Had she known of the difficulties that would be caused in the next days because of her sketching, costing her the contentment she was beginning to feel and changing the lives and futures of several others, Heather would probably have taken her sketchbook and torn it in half, then torn the halves into quarters. Heather was a highly intelligent girl, but she didn't have the slightest gift of prophecy.

CHAPTER TWO

Good Feelings Are Confirmed

Her bedroom hadn't been cleaned for the day. Dust puffs stirred along the red carpet and the polished mahogany writing table. Ignoring these, she reached for the sketchbook and pulled it toward herself.

It was her brother who had taught her that particular skill at Mother's urgent behest. "Gentlemen will be attracted by it," Mrs. Shaw had said when both were young and their father was still alive. "A female can play the piano badly or sing worse, but one who is able to sketch has a skill at which anyone can determine excellence."

Maurice, thinking of the high standards for art which were even then burgeoning in him, said, "She won't be much good at it."

"Somebody who knows how to paint and is in the family, my dear Maurice, is in a position to teach Heather this one skill and make certain that she *is* good at it."

Mrs. Shaw would never have understood that the two conditions didn't necessarily complement each other. As it happened, it was Mr. Shaw who intervened with Maurice and an agreement was struck.

Mother made it her business to purchase sketchbooks and saw that these were accessible to Maurice. She insisted on being notified immediately if there was any difficulty between the two of them, as Heather, she said, was terribly moody. It didn't happen to be true, but Heather liked being called moody. It sounded important.

Mother would make a point of strolling through the vicinity in which lessons were taking place. When fresh soft pencils had to be obtained in the middle of one lesson, Mother took it on herself to rush up to Maurice's room for the articles. That wasn't necessary, and it embarrassed Heather, making her feel like a helpless baby.

"Your sister will be able to sketch splendidly, dear," she said to Maurice, as if to mollify him for Heather's incompetence. "You will soon see for yourself."

Maurice sneered more vociferously than otherwise, as a result of Mother's pronouncements, or so it seemed to Heather. She drew a sketch of the Teviot River in full flow near its joining with the Slitrig, and in another sense she drew Maurice's ire as well. He detested her early attempt to draw the Buccleuch Memorial Hall. She was careful not to be in her hair-triggered brother's company when attempting to reproduce the image of a friend, but was rebuked for the action itself by Mother.

"Only draw nature scenes or gentlemen," Mrs. Shaw insisted. "Otherwise, you run the risk of making any female look older than her years, and it causes rancor."

Other reasons for bad temper soon manifested themselves as a result of her sketching. Maurice was furious at her clumsiness when she sketched one of the participants in the June Common Riding Ceremony at Hawick. His complaints on this occasion nearly caused her to have an attack of red-haired temper, as Mother called it, and strike him.

Through it all, however, she had learned. Nowadays, she was well able to elicit recognizable shapes and forms with sharpened pencils and sketchbooks. Not long ago she had done an acceptable drawing of herself with the aid of twin mirrors. Maurice, recalling his own ghastly failure at a self-portrait, had not spoken to her for days afterward.

Settling herself in the sturdy but soft slim-backed, padded chair next to the looped curtains that were pulled back to let in the morning sun, Heather opened the clothbound sketchbook to its first page. A new volume was being started. The vision of Julian's splendid features swam before her.

Just as she was poising the pencil over paper, a series of soft knocks were heard at the open door.

Mother stood in the hall, looking at her. Not for the first time

Heather had the impression of being observed by someone with a similar fragile skin coloring and bright blue eyes, but as short as Maurice. For the moment, as ever, it was profoundly disconcerting.

"I had no wish," Mother began, "to interrupt such thoughts as can be mustered by you at this time."

It didn't seem to occur to Mother that she was indeed causing an interruption.

"Nonetheless it would be useful to know when I will be able to venture out with you to fit the new dress."

Heather cogitated. Mother had purchased a double-skirt lilac silk with three rows of white fringe for her, the concatenation of effects bringing out Heather's coloring. This new dress was to be exhibited at an engagement party given on this night by an Irish peer and his wife in honor of their daughter's impending nuptials.

Heather was in no mood to consider the difficulties of a last-minute fitting.

"At some time in the afternoon I will be able to leave."

With a forefinger she gestured upstairs, rather than add that she would be available as soon as she had once more been in the company of Julian.

"I point out to you, daughter, that much of the morning and some of the afternoon may be required before Maurice is satisfied with even the preliminary results."

Heather shrugged, prepared to wait out forty days and nights of deluge for another colloquy with the Marquis of Thetford. With Julian.

"I feel that we should leave at some time early in the afternoon," Mother said. "I don't expect any added difficulties, to be sure. Certainly nothing fresh will occur that cannot be minimized with one of Madame Blanche's needles or, if necessary, a special corset. Nonetheless, it is better to be prepared for emergencies."

Heather wouldn't have felt sorry to miss a function given by some Irish peer and populated by loutish London youth.

"And you do have an obligation to look your best in the company of Ambrose Pennymore," Mrs. Shaw added. "He is to see you there and you have promised half the dances to him."

"Ambrose!" If Heather's skin could have turned whiter it would assuredly have done so. "Not Ambrose Pennymore!"

"You made a promise to him," Mrs. Shaw said implacably. "No daughter of mine would turn her back upon an obligation to anyone."

An unerring finger had been put upon the heart of this dilemma. Ambrose, to make matters even more difficult, was an amiable young man. Further, he was an unmarried native of London in good circumstances and decidedly fond of her. Given the least encouragement, an offer for Heather's hand would certainly materialize from his direction.

Ambrose could have claimed worthiness along with his amiability. Certainly he was an honest and wholly straightforward young man. All he lacked was the quality, whatever it might be called, that made any female think of a man as exciting. This quality it was his misfortune to lack in abundance.

"Of course," Heather nodded reluctantly, feeling a little ashamed of herself. "I cannot do anything else when, as you say, I gave my promise."

Mrs. Shaw beamed and looked relieved that the matter was settled. She had been arguing, as Heather well realized, for the necessity of honorable behavior. It was a stance which London mothers of marriageable daughters would not lightly have taken.

"Oh, Mamma!" Heather said affectionately, and ran to Mrs. Shaw to embrace and kiss her. The latter returned the good feelings, rising to the tip of her toes to brush her lips against Heather's cheeks.

Mindful of the need to remain alert for signs of the Marquis descending the stairs, Heather separated first.

"If I do not see you at the dinner table by noon," she promised, "I will make contact with you at one o'clock, should that be at all possible."

Mother nodded, confident that the minor difficulty, too, would be satisfactorily resolved. At the door, she turned and added, "Remember, my dear, you promised Ambrose only half your dances."

In the first glow of unselfishness, Heather was delighted with herself as well as with Mother. She would be doing what was noble.

Furthermore, the Marquis was unlikely to want her company from the moment he left Maurice's attic. It was more sensible to enjoy, if only briefly, such few pleasures as The City offered without Julian, the Marquis of Thetford, whom she had, after all, only met a little while ago.

Which meant her being with Ambrose Pennymore during at least part of the night ahead.

Considering that the banker was now far less likely to be a successful suitor, she found herself feeling more tolerant toward him. A smile crossed her features, and she supposed it was possible to take a few minutes of this wait in order to amuse herself. Drawing a sketch of Julian might be so absorbing that she wouldn't hear the man himself in the area. She took a decision with significance she couldn't have realized.

Swiftly she reached for the nearest hard pencil and began drawing on the first page of her open sketchbook. Such skills as she had acquired brought Mr. Pennymore's features to the page. She did not aim for exactitude, however, but sharpened Ambrose's prominent cheeks, lengthened the space between his gray eyes, and pointed the nose to a greater extent than nature had seen fit to do.

A sense of incompleteness would result if she didn't make it clear that the young man was possessed of a torso as well. There wasn't likely to be enough time for doing him justice even in a recognizable caricature, so she took another hard pencil and drew half a dozen lines to indicate that she was depicting Ambrose as a cherub. Fat legs and a hint of toes were sufficient. She reached for the soft pencil to shade in some image of a cloth across the nether part of him.

That was when an eruption on the stairs caused her to look up, the sketch suddenly forgotten. She dropped the pencils and book to the floor, noticing that the latter was open to this first sketch of the new volume. In her excitement, she wouldn't have cared. She ran to the door and then over toward the staircase landing.

In no way could she have known at this time what she had just done to herself and others of whom she was fond. With some two dozen pencil lines, she had wreaked more havoc than she would have previously considered was humanly possible.

At the landing she paused, determined to walk slowly as if she had embarked on some casual excursion. Pretending surprise because of the sounds on the stairs, she looked up.

Her heart was hammering at sight of the handsome Julian. He was indeed making a descent, but at a slower pace than needful. Possibly he, too, had been hoping for an encounter. She was aware of being delightedly examined once more by those deep brown eyes.

"I was hoping to see you again before I left," Julian said tentatively, unsure of the reception to be garnered by that admission.

She smiled cordially, considering it unwise to convey how happy she felt that he had indeed given further thought to her. At such brief meetings as had been vouchsafed Heather, a female was unlikely to be more than agreeable and courteous.

"I hope everything went well in the temple of art," she said, making casual conversation of the sort that could be expected.

"The sketching took a little less time than your brother might have preferred," Julian responded almost negligently, glancing down in some disappointment. No doubt Maurice had growled his impatience over and again. "However, I felt sure that it would be possible to see you once again before returning to the Lords at the proper time. I have agreed to join a debate on the subject of the Persian problem."

Heather knew little of politics and sensibly she cared less. To her, it was enough at this time that Julian was one male resident of The City who didn't try to imitate a Scots burr upon hearing her speak. A wide smile indicated her gratitude for that much, she hoped.

There was a pause between them, Heather unwilling to flout protocol for such meetings while Julian on his part remained far from certain of her true feelings toward him.

In the pause, it was Maurice who suddenly spoke.

"I will be at the front door, Your Lordship," said Heather's sibling, emerging from behind Julian and considerately descending until he was out of earshot. Not for the first time Heather decided that a more considerate brother couldn't be desired unless the subject turned to that of his vocation or anything to do with it.

Now that she was on the verge of speaking with him, as she had been wanting to do for so long a time, there was nothing more to be said. The Marquis had made it clear that their conversation must be brief. Little in the way of flirtatiousness could be attempted under so devastating a drawback.

"You had best rush off, then, Your Lordship."

To her mind, his reaction would prove what feelings he had toward her. A few idle words of regret and a furious rush to the door would mean that he had shown exaggerated social politeness a while back, and nothing more. It would mark him down as a young man who wanted to enrapture every female under the age of twenty-five.

"Yes, of course," the Marquis agreed.

Before Heather's spirits could sink at this confirmation, it was borne in upon her that Julian was indeed glancing toward the stairs, but he didn't move. Did she dare to hope that he had been so dazzled by her propinquity that his faculties were wandering?

"I have agreed to be at the—yes, the Lords—for a debate about some vital problem or other."

"Yes," she said, not entirely certain what either was referring to. The lunacy of speech without sense was apparently contagious.

"We must see each other again, Miss Shaw, if your mother will permit that."

Heather wouldn't have conceded under torture that she expected no difficulty whatever on that score.

"I will certainly discuss it with her, Your Lordship."

"Excellent, very fine."

It seemed incredible that she could have doubted his fondness for her. Julian was apparently a man whose new position in life had caused social difficulties which didn't always allow him to make his intentions crystal clear.

Her left hand suddenly seemed to be floating in air. For a moment she thought that the levitation was taking place of her own will. Realizing belatedly that Julian's hand was gently holding hers, she decided to permit the slight liberty and even to smile her approval. No reason presented itself for dissembling about her interest in this man.

"Yes," Julian said a little more loudly than usual for him, perhaps because he found silence difficult at this time. "I must run, or at least lope out to my carriage. It is on the street, of course."

"I feel certain that it is."

"To be sure, yes. I have promised to be somewhere else shortly."

"In the House of Lords," Heather reminded him, as the Marquis showed signs of forgetting this detail, which he had previously stressed in discussion with her.

"That's correct, the House of Lords." He frowned. "There is a very good reason why I am momentarily due at the Waxworks."

"For a debate, Your Lordship." Heather didn't find the recollection too easily come by herself.

"Yes, I believe that is correct. It sounds correct."

The bronze-columned clock on the lower level suddenly struck the hour, interrupting this exchange of ideas. Startled at the first peal, which sounded to him like somebody tapping a wet glass against the teeth, Julian promptly returned Heather's right hand to her control.

A feeling of disappointment coursed through her at the motion. She wondered if it had been reflected on her features.

Julian's warm smile, brightening his normally saturnine appearance, made it clear that he was aware how she felt about the interruption. The Marquis of Thetford may not have been socially adept in the purlieus of The City, but he was blessedly far from being a fool.

Secure in the knowledge that she would see more of him, Heather took a step back to allow him an uninterrupted access to the stairs.

Julian's face clouded at the prospect of her being further away. Moving forward he bent his head down and kissed her on the lips. Heather, accommodating herself to this turn of fortune, responded vigorously.

The last stroke of the clock caused him to pull back. There was a look of pleased astonishment on his features.

"I am not sorry," he said in a somewhat weaker voice than was normal with him. "I wish to make it perfectly clear to you, Miss Shaw, Heather, that I am not sorry."

Before Heather could say a word, the Marquis of Thetford was proceeding swiftly down the stairs.

CHAPTER THREE

A Sketch Is Observed

In the course of a passage of philosophy, some writer has petulantly referred to the slings and arrows of outrageous fortune. That philosopher, whose name escapes the mind of a fevered *raconteur*, had erred in favor of misfortune. Any older brother or sister of the gentleman in question could have taken him to one side and cleared up the misunderstanding immediately.

"With respect to this matter of slings and arrows," the older family member could have said, putting an affectionate arm around the shoulders of the erring *philosophe*. "It isn't quite the way you describe it in that little playlet for which you haven't been paid as yet. Good fortune comes first, and someone thinks that he—or perhaps she—is among the blessed. And then—mark this well, my boy, as you trudge through life writing epigrams for Dickie Burbage to speak as if he had a mouthful of stones—and then is the time when disaster strikes. Only then."

No record exists of anyone ever taking the errant thinker to one side and enlightening him. Nor is he ever known to have changed his mind. Had he been able to witness the happenings of the next few minutes at the Shaw home in Brook Street, however, he would have been a chastened man as well as an enlightened one.

Several tentative knocks sounded against the door of Heather Shaw's room. A female whose speaking voice was rife with local intonations called out respectfully:

"Miss 'eather, are you in?"

There was no response. As a result the door was opened by the aforementioned female, who was young and with dark hair, rosy cheeks, and merry eyes. She wore a maid's cap and a white apron over a black dress with gold buttons. With one hand she wheeled a hip-high cart holding two brooms, a dust pan, a bottle of Mr. Passy's Clean-O ("By Her Majesty's Royal Letters Patent," the label proudly advertised), a box of Mr. Passy's Furniture Wax, a box of Mr. Passy's Special Dustcloths, and an empty jar that had once held Mr. Passy's Perfected Boot Polish.

By the age of nineteen, Beryl Olton had been a maid for five years. Her position with the Shaws was the pleasantest she had ever known. Hailing from outside The City as they did, Mrs. Shaw and her progeny were not given to such local customs as harrying the servants. It behooved Beryl, consequently, to work harder than otherwise at the position in which life had placed her.

She looked around, reaching for one of the dustcloths. Her favorite mode of cleaning was to start at the farthest wall and work toward the door, then back along the opposite wall.

The mahogany table drew her attention first. On the way, she nearly stepped across something, inadvertently pummeling it with the tip of a sturdy shoe. It was surprising because Miss Heather wasn't untidy. The young lady had been brought up without a normal number of servants or a good income in the family until Mr. Maurice's daubs made him well known among the Fashionables in The City.

A book lay on the floor. While picking it up, Beryl couldn't help noticing that the pages seemed white and blank. Curiosity impelled her to investigate further, although she distrusted books as a rule. She riffled through the unvarying blank pages, careful not to smudge them. On the last of these—she didn't think of it as the first if this book was opened from the other side—there was a picture. Actually a drawing.

It made no sense to the eyes, and Beryl let a moment pass before realizing that she must turn the book upside down, as she thought of it.

Beryl knew that Miss Heather did some drawing herself, but only in a ladylike way and without the slightest wish or hope for financial return. Never before had Beryl seen the young woman's *things,* as she considered them. She looked at this example with what she felt certain was a wholly justifiable and even a friendly interest.

The drawing must be that of a baby, she decided, except that the limbs were too long. Modestly she averted her eyes from the sketch of an unclothed human being.

Compelled to look at the face once more, Beryl couldn't escape the feeling that it seemed far too well developed for that of a baby.

Only then did she gasp. That face was familiar. Having chaperoned Miss Heather on a carriage ride or two with the young man represented there, she recognized the somewhat exaggerated physiognomy of Mr. Ambrose Pennymore, the banker's son who worked at his father's enterprise. As if to flourish the artist's immodesty— Beryl tried not to think of it as indecency—Miss Heather had written her name on the lower right side.

Beryl closed the book immediately and put it on top of the mahogany table where Miss Heather usually kept it. She knew it would be unwise to tell anybody belowstairs what she had seen, but she did have a friend, a very special friend, who would be amused just as she herself was. The merry-eyed Beryl was sure that the two of them would have a good hearty chuckle over it. There couldn't be any harm whatever in sharing the joke with one other person.

CHAPTER FOUR

A Caricature Comes to Life

"Who would have guessed that Kerry O'Loughrane's daughter would be able to persuade a man to marry?" Mrs. Shaw asked her family in the gleaming four-in-hand carriage on the way to the Viscount's home in Clifford Street. "Not that Tessie is deformed or even ugly, but she *will* read those deplorable novels about Regency devilment! Oh, I bless the day that Maurice taught you how to sketch so you wouldn't otherwise waste your eyes!"

Maurice, looking owlishly out at the houses and shops along Savile Street as they passed, grunted by way of a response. He was wishing he could paint this setting and exhibit the result, but there was not enough energy for him to do so and continue that portrait work which brought in money for the family and himself.

Heather, sitting at her mother's left, sighed. The fitting at Madame Blanche's shop at Argyll Street and Regent had been entirely satisfactory. Under a dark cloak she was wearing the lilac with its white fringe adroitly placed upon the exterior. She had been unable to think for more than a minute at a time about anything except her feelings for His Lordship, the Marquis of Thetford, for Julian, and his feelings for her.

The carriage surged into Clifford Street at last. Box-shaped houses appeared under the February moon as if by magic, all with square windows and perhaps a finger's width of grass before each. Groups of men and women, braving the February coolness, were standing in agreeable conversation before the Viscount's home, as if reluctant to be entertained by the pianist and violinist which the Irish peer and his wife had engaged for this small dance-*cum*-reception in honor of his daughter and her affianced.

A knot of young men was planted some twenty feet from the outer stairs. Maurice, acquainted with most of the components from his nighttime peregrinations in The City, joined the group. Mrs. Shaw turned to her daughter.

"Every one of those bloods, every one not excepting your brother, has at one time given Tessie O'Loughrane a wicked novel. It would be hard to find a group of male Fashionables of a certain age in The City who hadn't done so, if you ask me."

Heather, about to indicate amusement at the idea of a gathering of former swains, was suddenly aware of a familiar form at her right. Another carriage had departed for the stables, leaving Julian Wyse, the Marquis of Thetford, to reach the house. He was dressed informally, in a white waistcoat, dark jacket, white shirt, and dark tie under a single-breasted overcoat. That particular choice of costume showed intelligence but not a high level of tact. He knew that a small dance like this one must by its very nature have little in common with a ball.

Heather spoke more loudly than she had intended. "I had no idea that *he'd* be here, too."

Julian turned. The briefest examination convinced him that no recriminations were to be offered because of that minor episode on the stairs in Brook Street. He smiled.

"My dear Miss Shaw and Mrs. Shaw." The greeting was impartial, but his eyes favored Heather alone. "How good to see you both!"

"Thank you, sir." Heather felt a little awkward at not having been prepared to experience his presence so closely. It would have been comforting at this time if she had, for example, put more kohl over the brows, thereby perhaps taking attention from her eyes. She was chronically deciding that certain features of hers were weak, and looking in the mirror during that recent *causerie* with Madame Blanche in Argyll Street had caused her to form the opinion that her sky-blue eyes were too close together. Further, they were the wrong color for highlighting her skin tones. In a week she would probably forget that grievance and make up her mind that the chin was far too recessive. Or perhaps assertive.

"Is my pictorial Boswell here, too?" asked His Lordship. Upon being assured that Maurice wasn't far away, Julian nodded and smiled. "The Shaw family, at least this branch of it, is perfectly represented."

Her smile of acknowledgment gave His Lordship the stimulus he was seeking.

"When you receive your dance card, Miss Shaw, I hope that my name will appear prominently upon it. Indeed, I hope it appears to the exclusion of all others."

"I would like nothing more," she admitted. It was quite beyond her powers of speech to add that both of them would be disappointed in that laudable desire.

As if from a distance, she was aware of her mother drawing a deep startled breath.

The reason for the latter manifestation became clear within moments. There was an apologetic cough from a man's throat, a sudden awkward chuckle, and then the new voice was heard:

"I do hope I'm not intruding."

For Julian, it was a perfect introduction to Mr. Ambrose Pennymore, a calm young man who was polite and serenely reasonable. His good qualities no doubt stemmed from his being the son of a banker who practiced his father's craft. They explained, too, why he had been shunned by young women seeking adventure, and flattered only by those who were willing to give up any prospect of romance in their future and settle for a life of unruffled monotony.

Had Beryl, the Shaw maid, been present, she would have chuckled at fresh sight of him. Heather's pencil had caught Ambrose to the life, barring the exaggerations natural to caricature. The pointed nose, the prominent cheeks, the wide-apart gray eyes, could almost have been transferred to Heather's sketch from the man himself. As for the lower portions of him, though scantly depicted, neither Beryl nor Heather would have been able to testify about their veracity, let alone their anatomical likelihood.

"I don't think I've had the pleasure of an introduction," Ambrose said genially.

Julian spoke with precision. Offering his own name, Ambrose was respectful. He had dealt with peers, but never conquered his feeling that they were different persons from bankers.

"I will say, Your Lordship, that you have found the loveliest girl in London."

The words were well meant, to be sure, but Heather felt herself flinching after Ambrose spoke them. Julian smiled at her, understanding the reasons for that particular response. It seemed as if no male and female had ever been as attuned to one another as she and Julian.

"I am happy that I have arrived," Ambrose pursued in the voice that always struck Heather as far too high, "before Miss Shaw could be swept away by so imposing a presence."

His words were meant with sincere flattery, as often happened with Ambrose. If he had stopped to consider his reason for being attracted to Heather and no other female he had known, he would have realized, perhaps, that it was her air of foreignness which captivated him. Not that Scotland was a foreign country, though it sometimes seemed that way, but Heather was different from the usual stuffy London girls with whom he had come in contact. He was not a fool, and he couldn't help considering that the London girls in his orbit were stuffy in the extreme.

"I certainly hope that I may have the very first dance in which you take part," he added.

Heather couldn't help shaking her head. "No, please, not the first."

Ambrose, as ever, was entirely reasonable. "Well, certainly the second."

She started to shake her head automatically, not wanting to speak. As her head moved, she became aware of Mother issuing a silent reminder. Heather had pleased the ingratiating Ambrose with a promise and could not withdraw. A woman's social honor was at stake.

"Yes, I suppose so," she said weakly. "Of course."

It may not have been a major triumph, but Ambrose couldn't resist looking sideways at the Marquis as if to indicate that it was the mere son of a banker who had triumphed in dealing with this lovely female.

"And one out of every two dances that follow, Heather, as you promised."

No stronger last words could have been chosen to elicit Miss Shaw's compliance.

"I will keep my promise," said Heather.

Julian's features didn't change expression, but a certain liveliness had gone out of him.

"It has been pleasant to see you and your mother again," he said levelly, almost as if the encounter had been as casual as it had been unexpected. "And to make your acquaintance, sir."

"The pleasure has been mine, Your Lordship," Ambrose insisted, genuinely believing it.

He glanced at Mrs. Shaw as if to confirm the knowledge of his triumph over a peer of the realm.

Calmly, the Marquis said, "I may have to take my departure rather quickly tonight, Miss Shaw."

Heather understood. Julian had no intention of being a witness to her dancing over and again with Ambrose Pennymore. She liked him for not being a good loser, unlike his overcivilized rival.

"Perhaps we can meet again at a more congenial time," she said, hoping that the words weren't making an effect of breathlessness. "At a time when your presence in the Lords isn't absolutely required."

"I, too, live in hopes of that eventuality coming to pass, Miss Shaw."

Was he being merely polite or did he mean every tense syllable that left his lips?

"Possibly we can, very, *very* soon."

Did he understand that she was discreetly asking him to call upon her at some time tomorrow? His features hadn't changed expression, not showing pleasure or scorn. She couldn't help wondering if he cared about a meeting with her under any circumstances, considering what had taken place here.

He inclined his head and started inside, where he would certainly pay his respects to the host and hostess and the fortunate daughter.

Having done so, he would leave. He would stride away from this place of temporary defeat, and there would be no expression whatever on his handsome face.

The balance of the evening passed, somehow. Ambrose seemed so delighted by Heather's presence in his arms that he apparently felt he was the most important man in this large room.

Some of the watchers wondered if Ambrose wasn't above himself because the Scots lass had proved as knowing as Tessie O'Loughrane herself. It was a thought that was dismissed on this occasion, but it would be remembered forcefully at different times over the next weeks.

CHAPTER FIVE

A Promise Made, A Trust Shattered

Determined to keep the secret though she was, Beryl took advantage of an evening out so as to place herself in the greatest possible temptation to give it away. This she accomplished almost as soon as the Shaws had left the house. She embarked on a brisk walk over to the home of Ambrose Pennymore's parents and their staff.

The Pennymore family had rooted itself in a four-story square-windowed brick house in a cul-de-sac just off Garrick Street and near Bedford Row. A dozen highly polished stairs on the south side of this unimposing structure took her to the staff entrance. She knocked and was welcomed by the tweeny, who curtsied respect-fully, as was due a full-fledged servant, and stood aside. In the small servant room, Mr. Gateshead rose to greet her.

He was a tall man with sparse blond hair. The smile on his fea-tures was genuine and welcoming, as was to be expected. Beryl was a friend he had met a mere month ago when she had accompanied the Shaws to a formal meeting with the Pennymores, a meeting held at Ambrose's bemused insistence. Gateshead, unlike the young mas-ter, had always been most popular with the ladies. If he ever mar-ried, the event would probably cause broken hearts from Maida Vale all the way to Bognor Regis, as he occasionally told himself only partly in jest.

"I hope that all goes well with you, Miss Olton," he began in the rumbling voice Beryl often found herself longing to hear.

"Thank you, Mr. Gateshead," she murmured, wondering what he would say if she told him about Miss Heather's drawing of Mr. Ambrose Pennymore. Only then did she realize that her desire to gain this man's interest had exposed her to a trap of sorts. She succeeded in not thinking too much about that.

Very often her head was filled with thoughts of the bass-voiced and handsome butler. She wondered if she was in love with him, and whether she would like to make him contented with or without the security of marriage. Instinctively she knew that the level-headed Norman wouldn't leave a family as Beryl's father had done and as her mother had in time been forced to do. There was a special security in Norman Gateshead's company. Small wonder she had purchased a blue flannel dress trimmed with narrow flat soutache for alternate visits with him.

On his part, Gateshead was sufficiently experienced to guess that Miss Beryl Olton was possessed of a fine figure under those concealing garments. To cajole her for a slap-and-tickle would be to get it. All the same, Gateshead wouldn't embark on some affair with a girl for what he was certain would be her first time, not unless he married her afterward. It would never have occurred to him that the innocent Beryl fretted at his probably having some other girl for what she discreetly thought of as a lie-down, and enjoying her own company only on more social occasions.

A place was cleared for her at the large table. The Pennymore cook, an imposing woman, resumed the anecdote she had been retailing about some incident involving Sir Samuel Fitton, the knight who was the owner of an enterprise which couldn't be mentioned in mixed company. There was a pause during which it was irritably explained to the cook's helper that Sir Samuel was a manufacturer of earth closets. The cook concluded her anecdote at last, and judicious comment followed.

Interruptions came in the form of summonses from the family by way of the bells. Because of his guest, Mr. Gateshead sent other staff to deal with the older Pennymores. The cook, left alone with the butler and his guest, rose from the table and joined her helper in her own domain, the kitchen.

"I take it that your family is at the O'Loughrane dance," Norman Gateshead rumbled. "I appreciate your visit, Beryl, indeed I do."

The young woman's heart pounded at a quicker rate than usual. Gateshead turned, busying himself with instructions to the parlormaid about bringing a toddy to Mr. Pennymore. He was in conversation long enough for Beryl to wonder if the two were close friends. It was an injustice she was doing Gateshead, but in no way could she have known that.

Hoping to gain his attention when he turned back, she said shyly, "I could tell you something interesting if you were nice to me."

" 'Interesting,' eh?" There was a smile in his voice, although it didn't seem that he was contemptuous of her maneuver. "I can't think what it might be in a house with two women and somebody who paints pictures."

"Ah, but there are artists and artists," Beryl said with purposeful ambiguity.

"There can't be the least excitement about painting."

"It depends on what an artist draws," Beryl said, looking down but confident that she had finally captured his interest.

In this she was correct. Norman Gateshead was no more or less delighted by gossip than other humans. There is something irresistible to even the most generous soul about the foibles of those in a more influential class. No doubt the tweeny relished anecdotes involving the servants upon whom she waited, just as the full-fledged servants were enthralled by news of the less-than-Olympian doings of the mighty.

"How do you mean, Beryl, that it depends upon what an artist draws?" he asked quickly. It wasn't necessary to remind her that the others would soon be returning to the kitchen table. It stood to reason that she ought to speak quickly if she didn't want them to know what sounded like it might after all be of some interest.

"Miss 'eather—*H*eather, she went an' drew a sketch of your Mr. Ambrose."

Gateshead looked as if he was going to sharply correct the assumption that Mr. Ambrose Pennymore was his personal property. He seemed undecided whether or not to retain the slightest interest in this anecdote.

"Well, there's nothing to surprise anyone in that," he said eventually. "Mr. Ambrose, he's fond of her and she probably wonders what is to be done about him. I would suppose that she drew a sketch to help her decide whether or not to encourage him into offering for her."

"So that's what you'd suppose, is it?" Beryl tossed her dark hair disdainfully. "For your information, Norman Gateshead, she drew him on purpose as if he was a babe-in-arms."

"An infant, you mean?"

"As good as."

She had told the secret it had seemed imperative to keep as her own. For a moment she didn't have the least regret in having been so forthcoming with him. If a man could persuade a female into a verbal indiscretion, there must be no limits to what else he could do. Considering the implications of that thought, the respectably-bred Beryl flushed to the tips of her ears.

"Do you mean to say that for the purposes of the drawing to which you allude, for these purposes alone, that she dressed Mr. Ambrose in swaddling clothes?"

"No clothes at all is more like it," Beryl said, looking away as if she didn't care to see his response to this appalling news.

During the next few moments, there was a cascade of interruptions. The parlormaid returned, claiming that Mr. Pennymore urgently wanted to see his butler. Reluctantly, Mr. Gateshead stood and frowned down at his guest.

"Not a word out of you till I come back," he insisted, in a voice that was so deep it might have been coming from the other end of a rain barrel.

"What is *that* about?" the parlormaid asked, hands on hips as she looked down at Beryl.

"I've been talking of something to Mr. Gateshead. A personal matter." It was quite true, of course, as she again realized too late.

The parlormaid took it upon herself to wreak a petty vengeance against Beryl and to frighten the tweeny at the same time. The latter happened to be passing from one cubicle to the next.

"Adele, you'd better get out of that uniform," she snapped. "The young lady 'ere is taking your situation."

Beryl started to say quickly that it wasn't so. The tweeny was looking at her without anger or fear, however.

"Too tight," she decided, referring to the dark blue dress and cap that were her badge of office. "She can't wear 'em."

"It's just a matter of letting out a few seams."

"Couldn't walk in 'em," the tweeny said. "Be a rare old takin' on, there would, if Mr. Gates'ead wants to spend for extra dresses. 'Is worship Mr. Pennymore's face will split, it will."

Her confidence was so serene that Beryl didn't have to make any interruption whatever. For that much she felt grateful. The tweeny smiled encouragingly at Beryl, as if to say that not every girl was so lucky as to fit into the Pennymore uniform. She walked out and up the back stairs, presumably to those attic cubicles which were used by the servants as sleeping quarters.

Gateshead returned in a few minutes. Beryl, who was expected home by twelve o'clock and hadn't wanted to wait much longer, smiled. It was impossible to tell whether or not the butler's feathers had been ruffled by his interview with the elder Mr. Pennymore. He looked impassively at the parlormaid, who glided away.

"Now see here, Beryl," he said quietly, resuming the conversation at that point where circumstances had forced him to desist. "Do you tell me that Mr. Ambrose, in the sketch that you have made reference to, is shown in the—ahem!—the altogether?"

"Not a stitch on him, that's 'ow 'e's shown!"

"Did you bring the particular sketch with you?"

"Certainly not." She felt bound to offer a mitigating circumstance by way of justifying that course. "It's part of a book."

"Do you mean that your young mistress defaces books?"

"Not real ones." Beryl cleared her throat, made a little uncomfortable by even a conversation about volumes of any sort. "It's a book of blank sheets except the one with that picture on it."

"You are referring to the picture of Mr. Ambrose in the altogether and as a baby." Gateshead had lowered his voice one more time. There was a light of glee in his neutral gray eyes. "*Could* you bring it over?"

"I don't see 'ow," Beryl said stiffly.

She was being asked to steal—there was no other word for it—something that belonged to Miss Heather, to a young mistress who had always been kind to her. Against that, however, one had to place the fact that Miss Heather didn't look back to drawings once she had made them. They went into a volume and in time it was put away on a shelf in her room and never seen again. If one particular drawing were taken, causing Norman Gateshead to feel pleasure, it couldn't be called a theft. She was simply permitting a good friend of hers to enjoy some special work of art.

"All that you would have to do," Gateshead proceeded, unaware that he had already reached his goal, "is to cut the sketch out of the book. Do it neatly enough and the young woman will never recall it was there in the first place."

Beryl thought it behooved her to make one condition before giving in. "You won't show it here?"

"Absolutely not," Norman Gateshead promised firmly. "I'll show it to myself."

Later on, Beryl would wish he had added the words, *and no one else.* Not the slightest repercussion, she was certain, would then have followed her friendly act.

"Well, I can't get away every night—and indeed, I ought to be starting back now if I want to arrive at 'ome by twelve—but I will try."

"Splendid," Gateshead beamed. "Absolutely splendid."

CHAPTER SIX

Crossing the Boundary

A note from Julian Wyse, the Marquis of Thetford, reached Heather before eleven o'clock on the following morning. In a decisive handwriting, Julian asked to take her for a carriage ride and offered to call at Brook Street shortly before two in the afternoon.

"Is it possible that he means to suggest making an offer already?" Mrs. Shaw asked, ever the hopeful one. Heather, as a dutiful daughter, had brought the missive to Mamma's quarters for a detailed consideration.

"I don't think so." She felt that it would be difficult to show any regard for a man who made a decision in such a far-reaching matter after nothing more than the impulse to do so. Possibly she had underestimated his feelings of loneliness in The City, as an outlander like herself.

"We must consider how to dress you," Mrs. Shaw said. "Unfortunately, Maurice is occupied or I would consult with him. Your brother's sense of coloring is magnificent, as we know."

Heather chose not to remind Mamma that Maurice was occupied with a portrait, returns from which would help fill the family coffers. Nor did she add that Mamma had paid no attention to Maurice's judgment when it came to the matter of furnishing their home. As long as Heather was unmarried, it seemed, she would have to withhold making comments about such disparities between thought and action. Not for the first time she envied her brother the freedom with which he spoke about whatever issue stirred his emotions.

It was eventually decided by Mamma that Heather would wear a box-pleated skirt and blouse in Napoleon blue satin and a tasseled cape to match. Heather happened to be currently certain, once again, that her sky-blue eyes were the very weakest feature of her face, a conviction which never lasted longer than others in that line, and she welcomed a chance to minimize them, as she hoped, by garb that she considered striking. She insisted, however, upon comfortable laced shoes rather than the kind in which she always had to leave the first two buttons undone.

Julian materialized shortly before two, smiling in a hesitant way as if he wasn't certain of his welcome. Maurice, well rehearsed by his female relatives, greeted him. There was some masculine discussion about the work that Julian would be doing for His Lordship at the next sitting.

Mrs. Shaw joined the males during the wait for Heather, who was following parental instructions by counting to one hundred as soon as Mrs. Shaw disappeared from her daughter's view. Only with this less-than-awesome task completed did she walk down the stairs and into the circular hall. Along the way, she was well aware that His Lordship had looked up to see her, and that only with difficulty was he able to focus on Maurice or Mrs. Shaw.

"How good to see you, Miss Shaw," Julian said, taking her hand and bowing stiffly over it. Heather, galvanized by the touch of this handsome black-haired man, had to keep from drawing a deep breath audibly.

"I look forward to a delightful afternoon," she said.

Julian chafed visibly at the need to discourse with others for even a while longer. *Au 'voirs* were finally broached and then made.

Heather found herself in His Lordship's company on Brook Street on a sunless afternoon. His Lordship's carriage awaited. Heather offered a nod up at Beryl, who was seated beside Julian's coachman. The maid would be acting as chaperone although the term was unlikely to be used. Beryl, unhappy as had been her wont for the last day, smiled with difficulty.

"Your carriage is a lovely contrivance," Heather said as Julian escorted her toward the brougham. Praise of a man's equipage was nearly always enough to please any Londoner.

The same rule apparently held true for emigrants from Norfolk. Julian positively beamed in gratification.

"Nothing better is available from Offord's of Wells Street," he said, helping her inside. "The framework is English ash and the panels are mahogany from Honduras. The footboards are American ash and similar pine for the roof. Jamaican lancewood is used in the shafts and Canadian hickory for the wheels. The spokes, of course, are of the best oak."

He didn't have to say that the oak was a home-grown product.

Heather felt dazed by the inventory. It would be correct to express further admiration, as if Julian had built the contrivance with his own hands.

"I hope that last night's proceedings were pleasant for you," he said after the carriage had got underway with a great barrage of noise.

"Thank you." Indicating that she had enjoyed the dance would be on a level with saying that he hadn't been missed. Verbally she walked a hairline. "The occasion could have been more pleasant for me."

"I felt that I would be a stranger at the revels, Miss Shaw."

"I thought that London gentlemen would always extend a hand in friendship to a wealthy arrival."

Julian considered. He was apparently a young man without any great gift for the small talk of Londoners. Not for him was the pleasure of circling around a point to be discussed without saying directly what was on his mind. In his native Norfolk, presumably, any young man enamored of some local female would simply take her to his breast at first meeting and pour kisses onto her lips.

"It's the women of London who are hesitant." Julian frowned. "I was given to understand that London women fawn upon men, and virtually dragoon them into closer relations."

"Perhaps those who said so were exaggerating in some cases."

"Of course," he agreed almost irritably, as if she didn't understand his recent words. "Look at yourself, Miss Shaw, going into last night's dance prepared to give your attention to an old friend who appears at the last minute."

She chose not to remark that a promise to Ambrose Pennymore had been elicited and accepted in the past. Pleasing though it was that he remained keenly interested in her, she would have hoped that he could bring himself to be a little less direct. It wasn't an objection she had ever anticipated in dealing with a man, but this one seemed to ignore all the pleasures of (dare she think it?) courtship.

During the last minutes she had noticed out of the corner of an eye that the coachman was avoiding traffic congestion by moving in the opposite direction in several crises. No other explanation could have been offered for his crossing Blackfriars Bridge for Long Lane, then charging into Bermondsey. The coachman turned back apologetically because he had taken them into a lower-class area, his double-breasted yellow greatcoat heaving as he raised a hand.

Turning to go back, he found himself impeded by a dispute between the driver of a hay wain and a cabman in tilted black hat and many-colored scarf over much of a scrawny throat. Each was vociferously demanding the right of way.

"One cannot expect an unmarried female to be unvaryingly consistent," she said, speaking a little more loudly so as to avoid hearing the conversation between angry drivers.

"True enough," he agreed, lips turned down briefly. "I am most pleased that you are here, Miss Shaw. Most pleased."

"You mean so that I can witness this dispute in the street?"

"Certainly not." He sat back, looking at her almost as if for the first time. "You are vexing me on purpose, Miss Shaw. There is some amusement for you, I believe, in doing so."

His frankness was disconcerting. No doubt he had also spoken pointedly in the House of Lords during yesterday's important debate about something or other in Persia or some similar foreign country.

Rather than offering a few well-chosen epigrams about the nature of woman, Heather turned to look out the window away from those who were quarreling. Her eyes encountered a house that seemed to have been made with dirty bricks as if to match ever-dirty windows. Children of the lower class, all of them looking no larger than some table decorations, ignored the fractious elders and played their games.

"Most of life is before them," she said quietly.

"True, but they'll never rise in the world, most of them," Julian responded, his mood altering to fit hers. "Their position at birth will keep them down, and so will their lack of education."

Heather was startled, not having considered the matter before.

Julian added, "They will have to work in situations of the sort that impoverished their parents, and always be afraid of losing the little that they have. Those with the mental capacity and ambition that could have carried them to greater heights, those people will be forever thwarted in most cases. For them, male and female alike, the poverty is nothing less than tragic."

That brooding tone in Julian's strong voice proved how much his own fierce desire to win at every competition was making him keenly alert to the deprivation of others.

The coachman was making sounds consistent with an imminent departure. Shouting in the street had come to a halt. No doubt the *contretemps* had been concluded in a manner satisfactory for the combatants.

Heather said with sudden urgency, "Stop him, please!"

Julian tapped three times against the panel closest to the coachman. After the carriage came to a halt, Julian turned inquiringly toward her.

Heather, as might have been expected, saw only the images before her and no longer gave thought to their meaning at all. Disregarding Mamma's celebrated dictum that a gentleman should be sketched in flattering terms, she felt her right hand almost itching to hold a pencil.

"I would like to sketch this scene."

Julian sounded startled. *"This?"*

"Certainly. It moves me, and I think an image of it is worth preservation."

"You haven't brought a sketching book."

"True enough." She turned back slowly. "I would like to return with such a book and a number of pencils to accomplish the task."

"I feel certain it can all be arranged."

"Several afternoons would be required before I am able to capture the entire effect."

"Ah." He understood now that something else had been on her mind along with the desire to prostrate herself before a temple of art. "I would be honored if I were permitted to offer the means for you to do so."

From his point of view, she supposed, it was an uneasy compromise with the rituals of courtship. He would have preferred to immediately offer himself along with the carriage. This way, he was bowing to her implicit wish.

"I can make myself and the carriage available for the next few afternoons, to be sure," he said. "There are several vital debates being held in the Lords, and some business that might strongly affect the course of Empire. But England has proceeded without my aid and counsel for these many years, and a few more days will be of little importance to Bulldom in the great scheme of life."

"I am honored by Your Lordship's desire to indulge a woman's whim."

He clamped his lips shut, rather than say out of hand that his interest in her was very great. The words didn't actually need to be spoken now.

His hand reached out for hers as the carriage surged into Cobbet's Lane, east of the Plough Road. It seemed to Hester that not only had they crossed over to a different area of The City, but that the two of them had crossed a boundary line of another sort entirely. They had achieved a greater understanding of one another. Smiling, she held out a hand toward him.

CHAPTER SEVEN

A Work of Art Is Appreciated

Beset by qualms on a scale previously unknown to her, Beryl Olton arrived at the servants entrance of the Pennymore home on Sunday night. For once, her face looked a watery gray in color that Maurice Shaw would have found interesting, and she had developed a tendency to peer over a shoulder as if dark forces were in pursuit of her and gaining.

Norman Gateshead, having descended from a brief professional call upon Mr. Ambrose Pennymore, welcomed her with a smile and walked with her into the alcove where they met whenever she called on him. Other members of the domestic staff took pains to give them a wide berth.

"Did you bring it?" he asked quietly.

By way of answer, she fished the folded sheet out of her reticule and passed it across.

Gateshead's eyes sparkled and his lips opened wide, but he suddenly put a hand over them. He was rocking back and forth in silent laughter. Had any of the staff seen him at this juncture, it would have been a death-blow to his ability to keep them respectful and slightly in awe of his usually magisterial demeanor.

"Quieter!" Beryl said almost automatically, although the only sound that had issued from him was no greater than that of steam escaping from a teakettle.

Gateshead slowly took the palm away from his lips. He put the paper down on the table.

Beryl reached out to take it back.

"Not so quickly, please." He was able to speak only with difficulty. "It is too good to—" Again the palm soared to his lips.

Beryl waited, not at all reluctant to have the incriminating material away from her person.

"From the waist down," said Gateshead, and he fell silent briefly. "She should never have signed it," he added, but only after he had once again recovered himself.

"Yes, I know." Beryl was more edgy than when she had come in. "I'll get rid of it right now."

But she reached for it slowly, hating to touch what she had taken by stealth from the house of her employers.

Gateshead offered generously, "I'll shred it to pieces myself, if you can't bear to handle it."

"Do it now," she insisted. "I don't want somebody coming in and seeing it by accident or any other way."

"I wouldn't let anybody on my staff take a dekko," Gateshead said sincerely. "On that, you have my word."

A bell could be heard in summons. The butler got up promptly and reached for his jacket. Recalling that Beryl had been unwilling to touch the paper, he put it neatly into an inside jacket pocket.

"I'll get rid of it later," he said, and kissed her on a cheek. "You're a fine girl, Beryl, a fine girl."

Beryl had wanted to wait till he returned, but some time passed and he still hadn't manifested himself. A long and complicated matter must have emerged, involving some service to a member of the family. It was time and overdue for her to leave. In truth she felt grateful that she would never again see that particular sheet of paper, that reminder of her own infamy. With her shoulders back and head high in the stance of a person who has nothing wicked to hide, Beryl left the downstairs staff quarters. Her right cheek tingled with pleasure at the memory of Norman Gateshead's kiss. She was a happy young woman.

Gateshead was kept so busy for the next hour that he forgot entirely about the drawing he had told Beryl he would destroy. As a result, it remained in his jacket pocket when he fell asleep. Monday morning was a busy time at the Pennymore *ménage*, with meals to be planned for most of the week and shopping orders to be made. This one morning, Gateshead had found, set the tone for an entire week. If all went well in this stretch of time, as a rule, there would be no fearsome emergencies over the next six days. It made little sense to be convinced of that, but his experience bore out the concept.

Monday was his afternoon out. More often than not over the last weeks, Beryl would join him, but she had to work today because of a small reception that the Shaw artist was giving for a valued client. In consequence, Gateshead was unaccompanied to the wedding at St. Savior's in the Borough High Street of Southwark. Two of Sir Samuel Fitton's former servants were to marry, after which they would be leaving for a new life somewhere in the Cotswolds, where the bridegroom would become a shopkeeper.

The nuptials were to take place at three o'clock. The retrochoir was being used because the Lady Chapel had been pulled down some five years ago.

There was no lack of color for the occasion. The groom's mother was decked out with her finest purple and gray and yellow. On her left shoulder there rested a bright green parrot.

"Gave me 'is word 'e wouldn't be anythin' but 'ushed," the harridan proclaimed in a voice that could almost have doubled in timbre for the organ that had been silenced by economics. "Cyril, 'e 'as respec', Cyril does."

The green parrot blinked an eye at Gateshead, who suddenly wondered if there were any guilty secrets in his past, and only then recollected that he was carrying in a jacket pocket that scandalously comic drawing of Mr. Ambrose Pennymore.

The groom's mother was accompanied by four small children and an irritable man who probably wanted to go out somewhere for a quiet smoke.

"I remember me own weddin', I do," she added. "Felt like I was swimmin' in jelly an' swore I'd never raise me voice again to any 'a the Lord's creatures, I was that 'appy . . . Alexandra, if you don't stay still I swear I'll thrash you 'ere and now right in the middle of this church!"

Gateshead looked away before the child burst into tears. His eyes lighted on Edgar Turnbull, the Fitton butler, appearing slightly less furtive than usual in a pitch-black suit. Turnbull was chaffing the groom and guffawing as he did so.

Somebody in the crowd, perhaps that brother of the groom's who was serving as best man, noticed that the Reverend Mr. Wilkinson was standing impatiently at the altar.

He gave a signal somehow for the bride to appear. Down the thickly carpeted aisle she walked, a wan-looking former maid whose red hair had been submitted to a constellation of side curls known as the French look, which ill became her. More importantly, she had borrowed a white brocade and satin-de-lyon bridal for the occasion, with a basque front and a square-cut neck. Mercifully, it was her composed but radiant features which drew commendation from all.

The bride was moving so quickly that two children, having been deputized to hold her train, couldn't keep up. One of them squalled briefly. The groom's mother and the thus-far decorous Cyril were at her side when she slowed down at last.

The groom, a step before his best man, reached the altar first and looked pleased about it. It was as if he and his bride had been taking part in a footrace.

The Reverend Mr. Wilkinson waited for the flustered mother of the groom to step back before he spoke, his words coming clearly if quickly. "Love . . . duties . . . responsibilities . . ." The phrases rolled off his tongue as though a carriage waited for him outside, sentiments made almost meaningless by the monotonous tone.

Gateshead looked impassively at the groom whispering his vows and imagined himself at the altar with Beryl Olton. A ring would make its appearance on the third finger of Beryl's left hand at this time, too, a simple circlet purchased well in advance and one that would never leave her possession. Then he would kiss her full on the lips and feel a stirring inside that could for the first time be welcomed.

He happened to overhear the brief colloquy between bride and groom as they walked up the aisle. The groom said wonderingly, "Being married, it don't feel any different."

"Yes, it does! It feels lots better," said the bride vehemently.

Turning away, his best wishes for the couple remaining unspoken,

Gateshead nearly crashed against Edgar Turnbull. The saturnine butler in the Fitton establishment had been beating a hasty retreat from the onset of happiness in his immediate vicinity. Turnbull looked like nothing so much as one of the dark forces that Beryl had imagined to be following her on the night before.

"I hope everything is well with you," Gateshead began.

"About as well as might be expected," Turnbull conceded. "At least I don't have to worry about new facilities in the servant's quarters."

He was probably referring to earth closets, with which any establishment of Sir Samuel's must be bountifully supplied. The master was, after all, a mogul in the earth closet industry. Most of Sir Samuel's staff accepted the taunts of their equals when necessary on this special subject. Turnbull, confronted by anyone weaker than himself, generally fought if there was even the slightest chance of the matter being raised in conversation. Norman Gateshead, as a strong-looking man with good manners, was treated with forbearance.

Gateshead didn't realize that Edgar Turnbull's customary gloom had been somewhat relieved in the last minutes. The latter had collected a debt along with interest at a percentage that would have made a usurer blush. Even when he felt contented, however, Turnbull looked as if he was getting ready to step on an opponent who already lay in the dust.

Gateshead, in a friendly mood, thought that it would be pleasant to cheer up Edgar in some way or other. Come to think of it, the means for accomplishing that particular feat happened to be lodged in an inside jacket pocket of his. Gateshead had offered his solemn word not to show the caricature to any member of the Pennymore establishment, but Edgar Turnbull was an outsider. The caricature amounted to a joke that Gateshead wanted to share with another, to see that other's eyes open wide in genuine amusement and surprise. He wanted to prove to himself that the sketch was so good it would cause even Edgar Turnbull to laugh heartily.

Aware of the need for some discretion, he gestured Turnbull to one side. The colleague, convinced that he was going to be offered a chance to earn money in some *sub rosa* enterprise, followed with alacrity.

"I have something with me that I want to show you," Gateshead began.

" 'Show'?" It sounded unpromising, and Turnbull wondered disapprovingly if he was going to be invited to buy shares of some aboveboard business in which years might pass before any profit materialized. "I'll look, anyway."

Gateshead found himself put off by the lack of enthusiasm, but none knew better than he did that one examination would convince the man. Turnbull had seen Mr. Ambrose Pennymore if only because the senior Pennymore's bank did business with Sir Samuel and there had been occasional meetings at the Fitton establishment.

"But you have to promise you won't tell anyone about it."

Making a promise was the merest of bagatelles! "Certainly I'll keep this to myself, whatever it might be."

"Do I have your solemn word on it?"

"If you want to show me this infernal what-is-it of yours, go on and do it," Turnbull said with what passed for him as sweet reasonableness. "Otherwise, stow it!"

"Then I assume that I have your word." Gateshead had been about to add "of honor," but thought better of that. Not allowing the paper to pass out of his hands, Gateshead drew it from a pocket and unfolded it.

Turnbull, having started to scowl, suddenly blinked and then looked as surprised as Norman Gateshead could have wished.

"Well, well." Turnbull nearly whistled. "And from the shoulders down he wears nothing at all."

Turnbull hadn't laughed, but a glint had certainly appeared in one eye at the least. Norman Gateshead didn't recognize avarice when he saw it, but sensed that his gesture had been appreciated.

"And the chit signed it!" Nothing had caused amusement in Turnbull as others knew it, but now his lips changed in thickness and it could be assumed that he was pleased. "Her name appears below, plain as paint."

Certainly Turnbull was more intrigued by that signature than by the caricatured features or the few straight lines below that proved Ambrose was being depicted as a baby.

"Norman," said Edgar Turnbull, rubbing his hands together and looking wistfully toward the pocket in which Gateshead had now deposited his treasure, "I have underestimated you. All these years, or for many of them, I have said to myself that Norman Gateshead may be a good butler, but his brain doesn't work quite as well as it ought to."

"I beg your pardon!"

"However, I was wrong, Norman, and I own up to it. All these years, probably because I didn't know you as well as I do now, I have been mistaken. I have not recognized a man of promise."

Gateshead was gratified, but modest enough by nature to feel that the favorable reaction, although there was much truth in it, may have been slightly excessive.

"With that particular piece of goods you are carrying, old chap, it is possible to obtain excellent results."

"What do you mean?"

"I am conveying to you that it is distinctly possible to earn money by the sale of that particular gewgaw. In the right quarters, of course."

"This? You want me to sell something that was given to me in confidence?" Gateshead quivered with unspoken outrage.

"That's what I felt sure you were consulting me about." Turnbull certainly sounded disappointed. "I can only say that I would be happy to cooperate and use my sources for a seventy-thirty sharing. By which I mean that you would gain 70 percent of the proceeds from a sale, as is only right and proper for having provided the merchandise, and I would take only the merest agent commission for my services."

Even if Gateshead had wanted to participate in such an endeavor, he felt sourly certain that he wouldn't see a bent copper of the money being offered by this particular source.

"I'd never do such a thing!" Gateshead insisted stoutly.

"Well, it would seem that first impressions are the right ones after all." Turnbull started off, then looked back directly at Gateshead for the first time. "Why don't you want to make a pot of money?"

Norman Gateshead knew that it would be inadequate to say he had promised the girl he loved that she would never again be troubled by hearing about the caricature. The worst objection that occurred to him, however, seemed like a more comprehensible answer.

"Because it would be unprofessional," he said stiffly.

Turning away, he didn't see the other butler staring after him in surprise. Nor did he see Turnbull's face suddenly reflect a thought that had furtively occurred to him.

The wedding party rode off in six carriages to the Pudding Mill eating house on Clink Street near Bankside. River smells could be detected by even the least keen nostrils as a feast proceeded.

Gateshead joined the others for the mutton soup and larded guinea fowl. With a dozen men he invited the groom to get away from the missus for a few hours during this evening. There were hoots of laughter at each invitation and each smiling refusal.

"Have a drink," Turnbull said, appearing at Norman Gateshead's side with a bottle. "Something I cadged from the house."

Norman didn't believe that even Turnbull would get away with an item out of Sir Samuel Fitton's cellar. He had probably purchased the potation somewhere. Sampling the refreshment took only a minute. Expecting a mild sherry, Gateshead was startled by a hell brew that could probably have knocked a navvy flat.

"It's rice wine," said Turnbull in light of Norman Gateshead's response. "Very much favored in China and Japan."

The taste of guinea fowl, which was served shortly afterward, nearly drove off Gateshead's memory of the rice wine. There was punch jelly that didn't resemble any color Gateshead had ever seen, and he wondered if he wasn't perhaps just a bit tiddly.

"Some more rice wine?" the tempter suggested, once again flourishing the bottle.

"Oh, I don't think so." Gateshead smiled in courteous refusal. "Thanks all the same."

He didn't reach for his glass until several moments had passed. Not till he gulped down the contents did he realize that Turnbull had poured some of that oriental concoction into it along with the innocuous red wine he had been drinking. He experienced the distinct and unpleasant feeling that the top of his head was detached from the bulk of him.

It was impossible to join others in discussing the recent wedding. Some guests felt that the reverend had spoken too fast, others that the talk had been just right in tempo. The groom's mother cheerily advised her son not to walk so quickly to the altar at his next wedding, which earned an icy look from the bride. Cyril, the parrot, apparently freed from the constraints of the recent ceremony and its trappings, expressed himself vigorously.

Turnbull suddenly spoke in Norman Gateshead's ear. "Don't you feel well, Norman, old top?"

"Somehow I'm not at my best," Gateshead thought he said.

"You should take something to drink."

"I did a while ago. 'Pon my word, I had no idea that the Chinese had strong constitutions. Nor the Japanese, I might add."

Turnbull smiled and nodded, but Gateshead wasn't sure that the other had understood one word.

"Here's a clean glass, old chap," Turnbull offered. "I just poured a little table wine in, if you think that's all your system can take."

Gateshead swallowed most of it before realizing that Edgar Turnbull had also poured some of the other stuff inside without saying so. He put away the glass as forcefully as he could. There was time enough for him to deduce (correctly, as it happened) that the brew wasn't any sort of wine whatever. Then he closed his eyes and knew nothing.

CHAPTER EIGHT

Love Finds Ambrose Pennymore

The young woman in the pale yellow muslin double skirt and blouse was pacing up and down the upstairs sitting room of the house on Bennet Street hard by Piccadilly. She was a blonde of no more than eighteen summers. A motherless girl, she had as a consequence accepted more responsibilities than others in her station. The house had largely been furnished by her, for example, and she took it on herself to be mostly responsible for her own and her father's relations with the staff.

It was this latter aspect of Clarissa Fitton's duties which was causing her the anguish under which she currently labored.

Because of a marriage and recent illnesses, almost an entirely new staff had to be hired. Clarissa had agreed to paying a new underhouse parlormaid five shillings a week along with keep. Nor had she protested at setting aside three shillings apiece for a new page boy, a groom, two footmen, and a carpenter. Each of these new staff was so suitable that Clarissa's concurrence with Turnbull's choices had been almost automatic.

Nor did she actually disapprove of Gladys Cannon as the butler's choice for a new scullery maid. It was perfectly clear to Clarissa, however, that Turnbull was keeping a more than avuncular eye on the well-formed young lady. Gladys must in turn have been as well aware of it as Clarissa, but offered no objection as long as she obtained this situation.

Clarissa could not escape the feeling that a cruel fate was destroying the young woman's life. In her distress she sought out her father.

Sir Samuel was ensconced in his study, writing on one of the many sheets of paper before him. Courteously he put down his pen on the wooden stand he owned for just this purpose and looked up.

"Is anything wrong?" Sir Samuel was a small man with hardly a hair on his head. His daughter's warm personality had not been passed on by him. Nonetheless she was the only living creature of whom he was fond, and it behooved him to find out what might be troubling her. "Doesn't the new scullery maid seem satisfactory?"

"It's that girl I want to speak of."

"What is the problem?"

"I am certain that Turnbull will be using his position to have his way with that maid."

Sir Samuel's face darkened, giving him the look of an angry orange. "You mustn't speak of that."

Clarissa persisted. "It would almost certainly be happening against the girl's will."

"I am busy at this moment," Sir Samuel said suddenly. "A bank representative is awaiting me in the large sitting room and I want to bring these figures to him."

"The girl has a drawn and wary demeanor, and Turnbull looks as if he owns her. The only reason she would agree to his demands is so that she can keep her situation."

"Clarissa, I see no need whatever to discuss this!"

"But it horrifies me to think about the way Turnbull could brutalize the poor girl, and do it under this very roof!"

Sir Samuel winced at the image that was conveyed. Had his daughter not been standing between him and the door, he might have blustered and left. Many years of experience with the strong-willed Clarissa told the mogul that she wouldn't move until she had perceived a satisfactory justification for his attitude.

"This girl knew the conditions of employment before accepting the situation, I am sure. A girl as comely as she seems to be, my dear, must know that the butler will be master in any way he chooses. In return, if she doesn't marry, she will have absorbed a craft to keep her until such time as she is unable to work."

"But it is dreadful that she should have to submit to Turnbull's odious attentions!"

"I am attempting to point out that otherwise she will be on her uppers," Sir Samuel explained, probably needlessly.

"I would like your permission to have Turnbull sent away, instead, eventually to a lodging house in Drury Lane because he'd be without a reference for other employment."

She didn't normally ask permission about any matter involving the staff, but felt that the current conversation between them had brought her to such a pass.

"If you do so, you will have to hire a new butler, Clarissa."

"For that task I am well prepared," she said fervently. "I can hire a very old man."

"I accept the likelihood. Ignoring for a moment the thought of a servant who is certain to be lumbered by infirmities of age, has something else not occurred to you about this alternative?"

"What do you mean?"

"Any new butler who comes in, no matter how venerable, will want staff people who are beholden to him for their situations. He will shortly be applying himself to weeding out the staff, such Draconian measures sending many of our retainers out to the street."

Clarissa understood her father's reasoning at last. A butler needed to be in control belowstairs so as to ensure the smooth running of a household.

"What, then, is to be done?"

"We must permit matters to take their course," Sir Samuel said gravely. "No one is a stronger advocate of morality than I am, my dear. You know that I have been careful indeed about who is permitted to be with you."

"Yes, Pappa," she admitted, eyes downcast.

"But we cannot truly enforce our standards upon the lower orders," Sir Samuel said. "Turnbull, for example, would make promises if he were confronted with the need to do so, but would then disregard them and instruct the girl to tamper with the truth as she values her situation."

Clarissa, falling silent, turned away. She caught a glimpse of a businesslike Sir Samuel reaching once more to grasp the wooden holder of his pen and heard that instrument screeching against foolscap sheets as she left his study.

She decided to go up to her room and take the copy of Mr. Trollope's newest novel into the small sitting room. Immersing herself in the woes of the fictitious residents of the fictitious Barchester would take her mind from this worst Tuesday afternoon in her memory.

On her way to the large staircase, as bad luck would have it, she encountered Turnbull himself. The butler nodded dutifully, but seemed unable to speak. His shoulders shook with suppressed laughter. His lips were thinned and he was trying in vain to cover them with a huge paw.

Not ever having seen Turnbull in such a condition, Clarissa wondered if he was drunk. Without experience of inebriation in herself or anyone else, she couldn't be certain. The butler was proceeding in a straight line, however, an unfailing indication of sobriety as she had gathered from the copious reading of certain types of novel.

Rather than glare at him or display undue interest, Clarissa simply walked. Impulsively, though, she did look down the long hallway after him. The butler was already out of sight. She supposed he had returned to the stygian depths of the house in order to vent his feelings of unholy laughter or joy, feelings which she found particularly horrifying in that immoral man.

"I—I beg your pardon," said the high voice of a young man, a voice she had never heard before.

Quickly looking over toward the large sitting room, from which the voice had issued, Clarissa saw that the double doors were wide open. The young man approaching them was alone. His far-apart eyes were gray, and he had a pointed nose that seemed to twitch in unhappiness. He was dressed respectably, with tightly fitting trousers beneath a tightly fitting jacket and a collar turned down over a tie that was loosely knotted so as to provide a note of purposeful informality. His reflection could probably have been discerned by anyone looking at his highly polished shoes from the correct angle.

"I do beg your pardon," Ambrose Pennymore continued, not moving closer because it might have been considered bumptious of him. "I wonder whether you will explain something to me."

"Certainly, if I can."

"Well, then, why—why does he do that?"

Clarissa brought her organizing skills into play. "You will first have to explain who is doing something and then clarify what this 'he' is doing."

"Your butler," Ambrose said, taking the instructions literally. "He laughs."

Disgruntled by Turnbull although she herself felt, Clarissa's first impulse was to defend a member of the serving staff before any stranger.

"Many people laugh," she said frostily. "It is considered a natural response to certain situations."

"No situation of that type took place in my sight," Ambrose somberly assured her, although it was necessary to raise his voice because of the distance that separated him from the lovely young lady. "I appeared at the outside entrance. I asked to see Sir Samuel and gave my name. That is all."

"You didn't by any chance briefly lose your footing?"

"I did not."

"Did you by any chance make a face?"

"I was as composed as I am now." Ambrose rubbed one of his prominent cheeks. "From the moment I appeared, the butler began to contort his features and then he doubled up. At first I thought he suffered from the ague or palsy, and went so far as to ask whether he needed assistance. My query seemed to change nothing. He was shaking, I can assure you, shaking violently as he gestured me into this room. While entering, I heard the unmistakable sound of laughter issuing from a man's lips. I realized, then, that he had been convulsed since he saw me."

Clarissa felt great sympathy for anyone who seemed deviled by the abysmal Turnbull.

"I am sure he was not laughing at you," she said soothingly. "Why should he?"

"My question exactly," Ambrose confessed.

"It will be the work of a moment to call him back and make vigorous inquiries."

"I am certain he would deny everything." Ambrose, too, was taking a logical stance, rather than letting the girl see him as an indecisive fellow. He wanted to be the only person to whom she addressed herself.

Clarissa, seeing cords standing out in his throat because of the volume with which he had to speak, allowed herself a smile.

"You might consider coming closer so that we do not roar at each other."

Ambrose was nothing loath to do so. As has been indicated, he found this girl decidedly comely. Unlike too many young women, she didn't pose as a helpless tool of circumstance but was willing to clarify difficulties and no doubt to help shape destiny to her requirements. Nor was she, like Heather Shaw, an outlander. London-born, she was a sensible girl whose upbringing must in some ways have resembled his own.

Now that he could speak without bellowing, he asked, "Are you Miss Fitton?"

"I am Clarissa Fitton, yes."

"I've heard about you," Ambrose conceded, although he had never been vouchsafed any information more than that such a person existed. "More's the wonder that we've never met till now!"

"Who would I have met?"

"Pardon?"

"Who would I have met," Clarissa asked, a bit laboriously, "if we had met?"

"Me, of course . . . oh *yes!* To be sure. I'm Ambrose Pennymore. I should tell you that my father—"

"I know." Clarissa was impatient of attempts to explain what she already knew. "*My* father often speaks of the Pennymore Bank."

"Favorably, I hope."

"On occasion, yes."

"Perhaps you yourself will be able to speak warmly from now on about the establishment and one of its personages."

Ambrose would not previously have conceived that he had in him the capacity to be so forward with a female to whom he had just been introduced, or to whom he had gone so far as to introduce himself. It opened up an entirely new side of his character, he thought, and felt proud because of it. His smile was what he would imagine might issue from a debonair Fashionable of London society.

If it looked different on his lips, somehow, more hesitant, he was blessedly unaware of it.

"I hope I will have cause to speak well of at least one member of that establ—"

"Ahem!"

The young people whirled around. That interjection had been made by Sir Samuel Fitton. The mogul had emerged from his study and proceeded down the hall to the large sitting room and a financial discussion with the Pennymore scion. In one hand he carried half a dozen foolscap sheets upon which figures had been carefully written.

At this point, it might be wise to pause briefly with the three participants in a state of embarrassment tempered by irritation. Some few words about Sir Samuel Fitton are in order.

The description of this knight that has already been offered, burnished though its phrases are, skirts the matter of Sir Samuel's temperament and of the influences that had made him the man he was. A clarification of this man's character is of importance to the tale, and follows accordingly.

Sir Samuel's primary interest was in the realm of his occupation. A manufacturer of earth closets without peer, of a product that was *primus inter pares* when colleagues came together for craft discussions, he had occupied himself by improving the merchandise even further. If he had an ambition, it was a selfless desire for every home in the length and breadth of the Empire to benefit from the use of Fitton's Earth Closets. Nor would he have been pained if the United States of America accepted the fruits of his and his staff's labors, even though the Americans had broken away from Britain. He saw the world as ready for this supreme manifestation of British skill, although it would be true to add that he had virtually given up hope of ever converting the Russians.

His wife had been carried off by the third cholera epidemic back in '52, leaving him with a daughter. Little Clarissa's further upbringing was entrusted to governesses and then to tutors. For the first time he had to take hours from practicing his vocation to concern himself with the raising of a female creature. What he discovered came as a jarring surprise.

Bright and pretty though his daughter happened to be, Clarissa
was often at daggers drawn with her little friends of both sexes.
Occasionally she returned from a children's party in tears. Drawing
her out on the cause of the difficulty required skills which Samuel
Fitton had not previously possessed about domestic matters. It took
rigorous questioning of the sort that Clarissa herself had recently
favored with the errant Turnbull, before Truth was made manifest.

It seemed that Clarissa was often shamed to tears when little
playmates pointed out derisively that her father earned his bread
and salt as a manufacturer and purveyor of a very special and particular sort of convenience. Sir Samuel's social usefulness had contrib-
uted hugely to his only child's unhappiness.

To remedy this situation became a major ambition of Mr. Samuel
Fitton's, as he was then known. His first step was to have Clarissa's
leisure time carefully supervised, keeping the child away from dis-
ruptive influences as much as might be. As Clarissa found herself
with so much time alone, she became an omnivorous reader. For
much the same reason, her skills as an arranger of her own life
became honed. Lonesome she may often have been, but she was
rarely pestered by sadistic equals.

Some three years ago it had dawned on Mr. Samuel Fitton that
his comely daughter must make a suitable and happy marriage. In
order to achieve this worthy goal, his own respectability must become a byword and closed to any question whatever. By making
contributions to Whig and Tory parties alike, he had seen to it that
he was eventually rewarded by a knighthood, the first step to that
peerage which he hoped to acquire as soon as possible.

Flushed with exuberance by this acceptance from influential personages, Sir Samuel made a serious *faux pas*. He wanted to show his
regard for the ruler of his Empire, but chose to manifest this in an
unfortunate way. It seemed that extensive repairs had been undertaken at Buckingham Palace, the Parliament having already voted
twenty thousand pounds in the cause of housing the expanding
Royal Family in comfort, to say nothing of the many important
guests to whom the Royal Family were required to give shelter. The
newly knighted Sir Samuel, then, wanting to be of help, sent to

Queen Victoria a gift of six of the newest models of earth closets from the Fitton line.

To his surprise, no immediate response from the Queen was forthcoming. The letter that he received after a time was coolly formal and signed by an equerry or some other minor member of the staff.

In pursuing his ambition for a baronetcy, Sir Samuel began to realize that doors had recently been closed to him. Little hope was offered. As he was nobody's fool, it needed only a minimum of thought for him to realize that somebody in the Royal Family, perhaps the priggish German who was Victoria's consort, had taken offense at a well-meant gift and was thwarting his every plan for social advancement.

Sir Samuel remained far from daunted. He continued making valued contributions to the Whig and Tory campaigns. One of these days, or weeks or months, he felt sure he would receive the baronetcy he craved, and from then it would be simplicity itself to become a Viscount. Perhaps he might even end his days as a Duke, causing his daughter to feel and show pride in her father's achievements.

But at the moment, as has already been shown, he was limited to the knighthood which had already been granted him.

Clarissa was the first to speak in the form of a sentence.

"I happened to see Mr. Pennymore in the large sitting room, Pappa," she smiled.

Ambrose cleared his throat several times. The courage he had known only moments back while in Clarissa's company and no one else's was quickly disappearing.

"Yes, that is correct," he said because he felt the need of proving to Sir Samuel that he was able to form sentences, too. "It is an honor to meet such a lovely young woman."

He was uncertain how he had gathered the courage to make so forward a statement, no matter how incontrovertible, in the presence of the mogul who was her father. Clarissa was looking down modestly.

Sir Samuel glanced from the flushed-faced young man to his daughter's gratified demeanor. It occurred to him that Clarissa was certainly old enough to have a male escort of her own approximate age, and furthermore that she would want one. Sir Samuel's major requirement for such a male was that he should be respectable and behave to his daughter as to a princess. Ambrose Pennymore, the awkward-looking young man whose father was beholden to him as a client, apparently met the primary qualifications.

"I have kept my daughter away from the tosspots with whom London is rife," Sir Samuel said, shading the truth with the dexterity of a successful man of business. "You aren't one of those tosspots, Pennymore, are you?"

"I, sir? Absolutely not, sir."

Another question was needed at this juncture, if only so that he would more obviously appear to be protecting Clarissa's interests.

"Am I correct in thinking that no scandal whatever is connected with your name?"

"Well, sir—" Ambrose was on the point of stammering.

"Speak up," Sir Samuel nearly roared. "Is there or is there not some scandal in your life?"

"Yes, sir, there is," Ambrose admitted miserably. "At the university—Downing, in my case, Sir Samuel—during the Senate-House final examination, I cribbed notes from one of the junior optimes, who was a particular friend of mine."

Sir Samuel, not having had the advantage of a Cambridge education, was unaware of the meanings of several terms used in Ambrose's confession of wrongdoing. He did, however, understand the drift of what he had heard.

"You were caught, of course."

"Oh yes, sir, I am afraid so."

The older man snorted. He could have guessed that a highly respectable Ambrose, confronted by the need to do something that he might have called *infra dig,* was certain to be caught. A lack of success at underhanded maneuvers, however, constituted an advantage in this particular situation.

"One moment more. This—this crib of yours, I assume, in no way involved a woman."

"Oh no, sir, certainly not!"

Clarissa, being well read, seemed on the verge of informing her father about the structure of university examinations of Cantabrigians. She could have explained cogently about senior optimes and wranglers in the order of university honors. Nonetheless, Sir Samuel didn't seem to be in a mood for welcoming further knowledge in this area.

"Very well, very well," Sir Samuel said carefully. "If you would like to call upon my daughter, Pennymore, you may do so with the proviso that a chaperone is always present."

Clarissa sighed in gratitude and relief, a sound which both men understood as they had doubtless been meant to do. Ambrose looked at her as if he had heard about females but not previously encountered one.

It was left to Sir Samuel, as that elder might have expected, to call the meeting to order.

"For the purposes of this visit, young Pennymore, you are calling upon me," said the mogul, flourishing the work papers which he had transferred under his left arm. "There is business to be done, and we shall do it now in my study. I hope this meets with your approval."

"Oh yes, Sir Samuel," Ambrose said swiftly in the face of the other's heavy-handed sarcasm.

Following respectfully behind his host, the father of the girl to whom he was so attracted, Ambrose gave no thought to any possible disloyalty to Heather Shaw. A flash of prescience had convinced him that Heather was fond of him, but her feelings were no more serious than that. He had been entranced by her, but it was blond Clarissa, the sweet and competent Clarissa, who was his true love. It was early days to think about love, what with his having just met her, but the formulation seemed proper.

True love.

He liked the sound of those words in his mind.

And he felt a moment's gratitude that he had never participated in any scandal whatever. Had he done so, he might have lost the chance to court and win Clarissa Fitton.

At this time in his life, Ambrose felt certain that he was indeed a fortunate man.

CHAPTER NINE

A Rendezvous in Public

"You cannot wear that!" Mrs. Shaw insisted.

As Heather was already adjusting white kid gloves, the comment seemed unrealistic in the extreme. She turned to face Mrs. Shaw, who had just entered the room to inspect her daughter's costume for the meeting with Julian. Indeed the Marquis of Thetford, as a nervous Beryl had just made plain, awaited her on the lower level of the Brook Street house, somewhere in the forest of pseudo-Orientalia with which the premises were infested.

Heather paused in front of the looking glass to inspect herself once more. The pale yellow antique moiré was satisfactory. Certainly her bright red hair, which she had now determined was a weak feature, would be minimized by this array and seem almost blond.

"It will do," she decided.

"Certainly not. You look like no one so much as like Queen Victoria."

Heather flushed. The Queen was *enceinte*, as it happened, with a new member of the family due to be arriving in April or May.

"No need for changing is apparent to me," Heather insisted.

Mrs. Shaw looked up with narrow-eyed determination at her daughter. "If a resemblance to the Queen doesn't please you, Her Majesty being married and you otherwise, you might consider that you would probably resemble my dear friend Maud at a sad time in her life."

Heather bridled once again. The name of Maud McThrapple, a friend of Mrs. Shaw's back at Hawick, was occasionally on Mamma's lips. The unfortunate Maud had been seduced and never seen again in the precincts of Roxburghshire, having presumably migrated to Edinburgh where her sins wouldn't be common knowledge. No one knew if the unfortunate one had borne a child out of wedlock or even been impregnated, but Mamma's tendency, in retelling the story, was to make a cautionary tale of it.

"Mamma, in the matter of these clothes which I choose to wear, I beg leave to—"

"Must I call Maurice in here to confirm how dreadful you look in that agglomeration of cloth?"

Heather was in no mood for her brother's company. No doubt Maurice felt the same way, being immured at the moment with a client whose portrait had been commissioned.

"Even if I wanted to make a change in my costume," Heather insisted, "there is no time to do so."

"Of course there is." Mamma turned to Beryl. "Go downstairs immediately and inform His Lordship that a delay has occurred and that Miss Shaw will descend presently."

Because of Mamma's insistence, Heather divested herself of the pale yellow and put on her forest green with the lightest trimming and an Irish-point collar ornamented by a ribbon tied into a bow. Mamma was deaf to protestations that Heather's hair seemed sundried by this alteration. The white kid gloves, however, remained suitable to her costume.

"Perhaps Julian will feel that my dedication to sketching has caused me to dress obtrusively and without my usual taste," she said, having refused to inspect herself in the mirror.

She reached over to a shelf for her current sketchbook. Something about the touch was disturbing. A look inside showed her what was wrong.

"The first page is gone," she said.

Mamma, having seen to it that Heather was suitably attired for the forthcoming great occasion, dismissed other matters with a shrug.

"No doubt you were dissatisfied with what you had wrought and hurled it away."

"I was ready to do just that, but I am almost certain that I didn't."

"There has been so much on your mind during these last few days that you must have forgotten all your minor actions," Mamma said soothingly after a protracted pause. "I suggest that you delay no further, but join dear Julian on the moment and continue to fascinate him."

The latter remark was entirely sensible, Heather decided. With the sketchbook and pencils in her largest reticule, she proceeded out to the hall and down the wide semicircular staircase.

Mrs. Shaw's *sangfroid* during the recent discussion with Heather had been deftly simulated and was far from her true feelings in the matter. It had occurred to her as a possibility that her son, Maurice, jealous of his sister's attempts at art, might have routinely made his way into her room and looked into Heather's sketchbook. Having done so, he might have sequestered a particular work in hopes of transferring its salient points to canvas. Because of her hopeful and sunny nature, Mrs. Shaw felt certain that Maurice's rashness would have stemmed from only the noblest of motives.

Mrs. Shaw had been warned on more than one occasion not to interrupt Maurice at work, and she was well aware of his imposing temper. In this circumstance, though, so upset was she as to feel nothing loath about disregarding his strictures.

Climbing the staircase resulted in no discernible loss of energy for her. Two knocks on the studio door caused the response of a muffled curse to be sounded just as she opened it.

"I know that you are painting, Maurice, but I hoped you wouldn't mind a brief interruption," she began cheerfully.

Maurice whirled around, his face purpling. To his mother he offered a stare of undisguised anger that would have surely daunted a less determined matriarch. Mrs. Shaw remained in place. Maurice lowered a brush without looking at it, then turned to the painting's subject. This was an Ancient of Days who was seated calmly on a snug-fitting chair.

"Please be so good as to allow me a moment's respite, Your Grace," said Maurice, speaking with the gravest difficulty.

The Duke of Rutland consented with a nod.

Mrs. Shaw smiled apologetically at the High, Puissant, and Most Noble Prince, as a heraldic document would style him, and led the way to the door.

"Now that you have outraged my client and myself," Maurice whispered with all the venom that he could muster, "I hope that your news is of importance and immediacy. Is it possible that our home is on fire?"

"I have no reason to think so, dear."

"Presumably there is no flood, either. Have we been visited by a catastrophe of any kind? No? And yet you have interrupted me despite my urgent and repeated proscriptions against your doing so. Might I now ask why?"

"If you will be patient for a moment, dear." Mrs. Shaw drew a deep breath to get the smell of paint out of her nostrils. She willingly endured the need to stand hunched over on the staircase, as no other space was available with as much comfort to offer. "Dear, I want you to tell me the absolute truth. Did you secretly enter Heather's room and remove a sketch from her book?"

For a moment Mrs. Shaw thought that her son was going to embark upon an apoplectic fit.

"I—did—not."

"You do give me your word about this?"

He nodded once, too angry to answer. Not for the first time he realized that his mother felt he was absorbed by jealousy of his sister's prowess as an artist, and only because she had surmounted one obstacle which had daunted him and he had been pettish about her success. He turned away.

"Thank you, dear," Mrs. Shaw said, and meant it. There would be no need to speak pointedly about any lapse which must never recur from this moment onward. Neither of her progeny, confronted by a possible misdeed, would lie to her about it. "Now go back and resume your work, dear, and proffer my most sincere apologies to His Grace."

Fortunately for her composure, Mrs. Shaw didn't see Maurice glowering briefly at her back.

Nor did she know that Maurice's subject, John Henry Manners, the Fifth Duke of Rutland, then in the seventy-ninth and final year of his time on earth, would live long enough to tell many others that the establishment of Shaw, the Scots artist, was most disorganized. The news would be a minor but impressive increment to the circumstantial evidence that was being gathered against the emigrant family whose members were busily conquering The City.

"If you like," said a delighted Julian, settling Heather into the back of the same discreet brougham that had previously sheltered them, "we can make haste over to the new Museum of Ornamental Art at Curzon Street, I believe. It is difficult for me to remember so many thoroughfares as London consists of."

It was a difficulty Heather had shared for many months after arriving here.

"Thank you, but I would much prefer keeping to the original intentions."

"Of course." Surprisingly, he chuckled. "Far preferable, too, to sitting in the Waxworks and debating the recent bad news from India."

Heather, knowing nothing of bad news and caring less as long as it didn't harm her or any British lives, occupied the next minutes by peering anxiously out the window.

Not surprisingly, in light of his feeling of fealty to her, Julian said, "I must tell you that I cannot remember where we went that you wanted to return to and sketch."

"Instruct the driver to hoist Blue Peter for Bermondsey," Heather said with contentment. "Should a more striking view appear I can change plans immediately."

Julian, somewhat disconcerted by so much purposiveness from another, accordingly communicated with the coachman, interrupting the latter in the midst of a brief monologue aimed at the abstracted Beryl. The maid was recalling that she had been forced to leave the infernal drawing with Norman Gateshead, and was hoping that he had destroyed it just as he'd given his word to do.

Julian's awareness of the withdrawn maid and irritated coachman caused some ruffling of his own feelings when he returned his attentions to Heather.

Forcefully, despite having warned himself to be the perfect gentleman, he said, "I have always wanted things to be understood
clearly, black-on-white, so to say. The hint, the unspoken agreement, are not easeful situations as far as I am concerned."

Required to pay attention to her host, Heather said, "You will
find a life in politics rather wearing, then, from what I have been
given to understand of it."

"Quite the contrary, I think. In political adventuring, no one's
statement is worth accepting on face value and everybody's indirect
remarks are worth even less. Until I ventured into the halls of Parliament, I had never been a cynic, but now I can spout aphorisms like
a singer in the Halls."

"Time will tell if your vision of politics is a true one," she said.
"Time will tell other things, too, as I had hoped to indicate in your
presence not long ago."

"Too long ago," Julian said so miserably that her heart went out
to him. "That is my complaint."

"I can see no other course," she said. "The passing of hours and
even days and perhaps weeks can better permit us to know our own
minds and not rely on the impulsive feeling of the moment."

He was startled. "Do you also feel at the moment that—?"

"I spoke, as it were, figuratively."

"Yes, to be sure," he said, relapsing into stygian gloom. "Not in
any manner to deal with reality."

He had led the way into a discussion subject that could have
occupied London males for any number of unproductive hours.
Truth to tell, she had no protracted inclinations toward theoretical
concerns, either. She was well met with Julian, but differing notions
of reality would keep her out of his arms if only for a little longer.

He fell silent, permitting Heather to stare out the window once
more.

Immediately she perceived what had happened. The coachman,
whose sense of direction was ill-attuned to finding locations in The
City, had proceeded in another path. From Abbey Street in Southwark, he had drifted through Long Lane to White Street, attracting
the envious glances of hollow-eyed urchins and their elders. These

sad folk lined the streets. Their existence was a source of irritation to most of the more fortunate whose coppers were not so hard-earned.

A large brick building, sturdily made, faced her. Its windows were broken. Hard use by the neighboring poor had made it into a dark stone shell.

"I was hardly expecting to see St. Giles Cripplegate," Heather said quietly. "But this is—ghastly."

To his great credit, Julian didn't urge her away or point out that the interest of a young woman in such a place was far from seemly. Drawing the attention of a whiskerando wearing at least two thin coats to keep warmer in the February chill, Julian raised his voice.

"What sort of place is this?"

The Londoner recognized intonations of an outlander, so he kept from a sarcastic answer.

"It's all as is left 'a the White 'ell," the native rasped in tobacco-thickened tones.

Julian understood instinctively, aided by one more look at the structure. "A prison, is it?"

"Was," the native responded. "Been thrun aht by the city 'a Lunnon, jus' like Fleet Street prison will be. All the 'igh class custom, beggin' your worship's pardon, will go aht to 'olloway, from what I been told."

Julian thanked the man and offered a copper, which was gratefully accepted. As it was being tested against the man's few remaining teeth to make sure it wouldn't bend and was therefore genuine, Julian turned away.

"*This* is the sort of shame we should be talking about in the Waxworks, not news of India," he said quietly but with strong feeling. "The Lords all think that people are poor only because of their own choices. Did you see the gnarled hands on that man? What kind of work could he possibly obtain?"

Heather nodded sympathetically. She would very much have liked to draw that fellow and would have paid for the privilege. Making a transaction out of such a wish would be unseemly, however, as if she was signaling him out as an aberration of the streets. She and Julian looked at each other in silent agreement about what they were seeing.

It was but the work of a moment for Heather to begin sketching the edifice and some of the figures at the half-open door. Julian watched over a shoulder, then compared her efforts against the reality. Heather didn't see his look of somber approval about what she was doing.

She sensed his impatience as she sketched on, and the work went more quickly than it might have done otherwise. At first she considered that it wasn't skillfully done. Looking at it once again, though, she concluded that the roughness offered the best possible reflection of the particular image confronting her.

Politeness dictated showing the result of her work to the host who had enabled her to accomplish it. With that purpose in mind, she turned. As Julian had retreated next to the opposing window, she reached the sketchbook across toward him, bending sideways at the hips to do so.

The last reaction she expected was for Julian to look at her contorted self and say vehemently:

"Do you want me to go mad?"

It did seem as if he found her position to be some sort of incitement. Wisely, she pulled back.

"Please answer that simple question," he persisted. "Do you, or do you not, want me to lose my mind and be carried away to bedlam?"

She decided to deal with him almost as if he had put forth a debating point in the Lords.

"I am frank to confess that I do not."

"In which case, I would deeply appreciate your refraining—no!" He suddenly swallowed. "I have no wish for you to do that, only to indicate whether you find me a companion worthy of you."

She felt that in the recent past she had made her favorable feelings clear by way of inference. Apparently Julian wanted a concrete response, an agreement in words. The sons of Thetford may have been desirable and intelligent, but they seemed literal-minded in the extreme.

"I am in your presence now," she said, not having intended a Delphic utterance because she felt it unwise to yield in this matter.

"Ah, but that is only in order for you to indite a sketch as you have been anxious to do."

She said quietly, "I find it difficult to be forced into considering these matters so often."

"In other words," he said in a quieter voice, having taken a deep breath, "you ask me to offer more patience than nature has allowed me."

"Truly I suggest patience for both our sakes, Julian."

"Not for mine. In saying so I speak from the heart."

Had he been in a different mood, she would have made some mettlesome remark about the curious method by which he produced vocal sounds. In dealing with him at this time, however, it was best to jar him no further.

"I assume, then, that your mind is open on the subject of my attentions," he added, pursuing the matter.

It was a mistaken assumption, as she had decided to encourage him after a seemly interval. His impetuosity was so painful because she had almost been made a pariah by other men only for being away from the area in which she had grown to maturity. Such extremes of response needed time to be accepted.

"My mind is indeed open," she said mendaciously.

It was her intention to dismiss the subject at this time, but a smile formed on her lips as she spoke the words. Certainly she was amused by her own tampering with the truth.

She had looked away from him, but heard the gasp that he emitted and correctly identified it as being caused by surprise and pleasure.

"Can I be sure," he began so quietly that he might not have been aware that he had spoken aloud.

Heather said instantly, "It is time to return, I believe."

"Of course, yes." It was saddening to hear his tones without the joy that had exalted him a moment ago.

A few words to the coachman were sufficient to start the homeward journey. No communication passed between her and Julian for a while. At one point she heard him saying again, "But how can I be certain?" Once more he had been entirely unaware of speaking his thought.

The coachman took a course that resembled none that Heather could have anticipated, although it offered the opportunity to see more of London than had previously been vouchsafed her. It was a cause of further gratitude that the errant coachman was not a ship's navigator.

By some method known to himself alone, the carriage eventually reached Blackfriars Bridge from the Bermondsey side. Afterward, Heather would point out to herself that the coachman must have been fully occupied by the task of approaching the bridge in the midst of heavy traffic. No doubt Beryl was watching the maneuvers and felt prepared to disembark hastily if the need arose.

Heather was aware of a stirring from Julian's direction, but found herself ill-prepared for his next move. It was the second time in their acquaintance that he kissed her. His lips were strong upon hers. She had no intention of responding, but couldn't seem to help herself.

Only when the carriage was securely traversing the bridge did Julian withdraw his lips and move away reluctantly.

"At this time, I could ask for nothing more," he said, but only after pausing and in a more uncertain tone than was customary for him.

Heather knew that she had unwittingly offered unmistakable confirmation of her positive feelings toward him. The sons of Thetford were indeed literal-minded, but on consideration she didn't always find that particular attitude to be objectionable.

CHAPTER TEN
A Reckoning of Sorts

Norman Gateshead had lived through the sort of Tuesday morning and afternoon that could only have been wished upon him by a foul-minded enemy. His head felt as if it belonged to a different body. His eyes appeared to distend out of their sockets and only by quickly lifting his head was he able to keep them in place, or so he thought. Both hands shook when he carried trays to various members of the Pennymore family, which employed him. It has been said on more than one occasion that the aftereffects of excessive indulgence in spirits are not cause for hilarity, but anyone observing him and presently unaffected by the malady might have found it difficult to restrain a chuckle or two.

Compounding his unease was the certainty that he had imbibed only moderately at the wedding he had attended on the day before. Greater unhappiness fell to this butler's portion when he realized that the caricature of Mr. Ambrose Pennymore, the gift of trust and affection from Beryl Olton, had disappeared. No longer did it reside in an inside pocket of his best jacket.

Gateshead was not slow to draw conclusions. Certain points were clear upon stringent analysis at a time when various organs had stopped their hammering upon his vulnerable person.

Point one: he had shown the sketch in question to a colleague, Edgar Turnbull. Two: said colleague, Turnbull, had suggested capitalizing upon the caricature by selling it, presumably to one of the newspapers which printed society gossip. Three: without drinking to excess he, Gateshead, had become ill. Four (and with this point it was necessary to expend the greatest powers of ratiocination): upon his recovery the sketch was found to have disappeared.

Gateshead was not given to tossing off pithy aphorisms in foreign languages, along the line of *quod erat demonstrandum.* If he had been, his speech on that miserable afternoon would have been unintelligible to the balance of the Pennymore staff.

Not till four-thirty, when he was more than partially recovered, was he able to arrange two hours away from the house. Bennet Street, where Edgar Turnbull lurked in Sir Samuel Fitton's establishment, was the first on the right as he turned down St. James's from Piccadilly. An even more unpleasant time awaited him than he had known while being sick, but no way of avoiding this session presented itself to his *amour propre.*

True enough, Turnbull was a man with a sharp eye out for new coppers and might have sold the particular sketch. But it was also possible that taking it in the first place was his colleague's idea of a joke worth playing. It wouldn't be the least surprise that Turnbull was afflicted with a sour sense of humor and took pleasure only in someone else's embarrassment and shame. That business with the drinks proved the point beyond any doubt.

Gateshead knew, too, that if the worst had happened he would have lost Beryl Olton for all time. It seemed impossible for one accident following another to result in taking away from him that maid above all others whom he loved.

On the top step of the stairs leading down to the servants entrance he saw that the door was opening. Turnbull, looking like a squire in panto who has just pushed his progeny into the snow for some minor infraction, stood with his jacket off despite the chill weather. Gateshead could see the ferret-faced young man who had come to the door. The latter was carrying a package.

"I've been sent by Quixwood's in Regent Square with the special order for"—he motioned at the package "—for the nipper."

"What's this?" Turnbull glowered, adding nothing at all encouraging to his looks. "What nipper?"

"You should know," the other insisted. He looked at the name written in flowing script on the package. "Master Sammy Fitton."

" 'Master—' " Turnbull sounded as if he was choking with anger.

"His father purchased a gift book for Master Sammy and asked for it to be sent over," the young man said fluently. "I believe that it is a book about Red Indians in the former American colonies, a book with many illustrations that should please a boy. At any rate, the store is owed four-and-six for this inscribed copy."

"What in *blazes* are you nattering about?" Turnbull asked roughly. His face began to enlarge with fury, or so it seemed from even a short distance.

"This book has been purchased and inscribed for Master Sammy Fitton," the stranger said a little more hurriedly.

"How would you feel if I told you that 'Master' Sammy Fitton is not only full-grown, but is a successful businessman as well?"

"How is that?" Now the other was genuinely taken aback. "If that is the case, I certainly owe you an apology." A look of suppressed anger twisted his features. "I owe something more to another person as well, I don't mind telling you, sir, a person who makes errors. That much I fully intend to repay. I apologize for your having been needlessly bothered."

Turnbull made a pair of fists as the stranger turned toward the bottom step, not wanting his prey to leave before a thorough dressing-down.

"You're a thief and a lying scalawag!" he shouted to the man's back, his own face purpling with frenzy. "I have a good mind to see you put into jail for this myself."

The stranger didn't turn to argue or plead. He did, however, increase his pace. To Turnbull, such flight from hearing an opinion like his must have seemed like the greatest of insults. He suddenly ran toward the stranger, reaching an elbow around the younger man's neck from behind. With his free hand, Turnbull hammered against the younger man's back.

Gateshead hurried down, prepared to help the stranger if only so that Turnbull wouldn't face a charge of assault. Turnbull looked surprised at the sight of him, but a quick motion with one hand signified that Gateshead should retreat and leave him to wreak havoc upon the ferret-faced stranger.

The latter, now freeing himself because of the distraction, whirled on Turnbull. A firm revenging fist crashed solidly against the left side of Turnbull's aggressively thrust-out jaw, causing the older man to stagger before he slipped to the ground. The ferret-faced man nodded once as Gateshead turned menacingly toward him, then resumed his flight.

Rather than following, Gateshead helped the fallen warrior get up. The extreme of dislike was fading out of Edgar Turnbull's eyes now that the malefactor had slung his hook.

"He helped you get even, didn't he?" Turnbull asked, not needing the answer, and rubbed his jaw. "I don't blame you as much as him. Ought to be up before a Bow Street beak, he ought."

It was an indirect admission that Turnbull had previously achieved some feat of double-dealing for which retaliation was only to be expected. Norman Gateshead, still hoping that the abducted sketch was in the other's possession, ignored it.

Turnbull, being led into the servants hall, was concentrating on the recent encounter. "Can you imagine that? A name is inscribed in the book, and then that plausible scoundrel goes out and collects the ill-gotten loot by representing himself to be delivering a purchase! The rascal!"

"It is abominable," Gateshead agreed sincerely.

Turnbull, however, was more deeply reflective about the episode. "Of course, *I* would need at least one other person if I would see it done effectively," he mused, bearing out the late Napoleon's estimate of his race as a nation of shopkeepers. "Half the lolly for each would result in a small profit, though. Too small to be worthwhile."

It seemed that Edgar Turnbull had also considered the scoundrelly enterprise to be one which he might himself have attempted as a way of earning additional money. As soon as Gateshead was aware of that, he began to accept the likelihood that the sketch he had come to seek was almost certainly no longer available to him.

Nonetheless he led Turnbull to the table in the alcove next to the ample kitchen. These surroundings differed in no major particular from the ones in which Gateshead spent most of his life. The faces of the nearby servants, however, were unknown to him. Ignoring his own indisposition, Turnbull waved them away with an imperious hand.

Norman Gateshead took advantage of the relative privacy to

speak pointedly. "I want that sketch back." It was best, he thought, to act as if he anticipated its return. The possibility still remained that he might be pleasantly surprised.

"Did you say sketch?"

"That was the word I used."

"What sketch would you be referring to?" Turnbull looked rather like an effigy of himself as it might be displayed in Madame Tussaud's on Baker Street.

"The one you took, of course," Gateshead insisted. "No one else would be so low as to spike somebody's wine in order to steal that person's property. At least no butler would. Some masters of different types, yes, but no other butler."

Turnbull, distracted, said urgently, "Lower your voice, for heaven's sake!"

Scenting an opportunity to exert more pressure, Gateshead raised his voice instead.

"I want that sketch back," he insisted. "The one you stole from me."

Some answer had to be made, as Turnbull was well aware. "I thought that the drawing was what you might call incriminating, so when it slipped out of your pocket I got rid of it myself."

"I don't trust you," Gateshead trumpeted. "I want that sketch returned to me so that I can rip it to shreds with my bare hands."

Once again Turnbull writhed like a creature in torment. "At least don't say 'bare' hands! Certainly not so loudly. It's indecent."

Gateshead, who had thought of himself as a juggernaut never to be deflected in his goal, was set back by the sudden change in topic. Turnbull as he knew him wouldn't have been afraid to curse in the presence of Vicky and Albert themselves. Aside from a certain *pro forma* regard for the sensibilities of his employers, Edgar Turnbull was not known to care about anyone else's feelings.

"What are you talking about?" Gateshead snapped.

Before he could finish the words, he saw Turnbull looking across toward the alcove door. Oddly there was a new softness in his features, the eyes wide, the saturnine complexion almost faded momentarily. He looked like a frog who had swallowed a lily pad and found it succulent.

Gateshead's eyes followed the other butler's. A girl stood near the doorway, a girl in scullery maid's gray uniform. As Gateshead watched, she was fluffing a lick of dark hair into place. Experienced with the fair sex as Norman Gateshead was, he knew perfectly well that the scullery maid was pretending not to know that she was observed by two men.

Turnbull sighed, a sound unlike any that had ever issued from the malevolent one in Gateshead's presence. It didn't require the statecraft of a Palmerston to realize that he was taken with the girl, and that relations between them had previously reached an intimate phase. Gateshead, who had never before known his friend to show the least effect of any passion he may have felt, except that for money gained in divers illicit ways, was astonished.

For it did indeed seem as if Edgar Turnbull, of all creatures, found himself both enamored and surprised in turn by the feeling. All of his friends, now known as his former friends, would be talking about it for weeks or months. If Edgar Turnbull could pause in his pursuit of ill-gotten pence to indulge himself in tenderness with a female, then it became impossible to judge anyone. It was as if the devil had suddenly decided to permit Faust to go on about his business and even gave out a cigar to promote additional good-will.

Nonetheless, Gateshead saw the opportunity to resolve his own difficulty with only a minimum of further ado.

"I put it to you as quietly as I am able," he said, obliging the distraught Turnbull, "that I am here for the sketch that you took from me by main force."

Edgar Turnbull reluctantly faced his colleague. There was no way to keep this news to himself any longer, even though it was a bulletin he would much rather have glossed over.

"Don't go up in the air like a balloon, now," he cautioned, "but I —I truly haven't got it anymore. I—well, I realized something on it."

Gateshead had expected no less when push came to shove, but found himself fighting a tendency to reel in dismay where he stood.

His opposite number, having revealed almost all, looked away, presumably in dread of being reminded that he had promised a seventy-to-thirty division of any spoils. He may have felt that he had already endured a sufficiency of pain and anguish.

Gateshead in turn wanted no physical reminder of what had taken place. "I suppose you sold it to one of the gossip papers."

Turnbull nodded.

Norman Gateshead could only tell himself dazedly and repeatedly that Beryl wouldn't forgive him for letting the infernal scrawl out of his hands. He had lost Beryl forever.

Without another word Gateshead turned and almost ran out of the Fitton home.

CHAPTER ELEVEN

The Culprit Is Informed of the Crime

Heather and a friend were sitting in the lavishly decorated Gothic hall used by the House of Lords, her interest far indeed from the dull debate about an amended Trades Union bill proceeding on the floor below. Nor did she spare much attention for the sight of the south end of this huge room, with the thrones of the Sovereign and Consort, the latter an inch lower. One look at the fabled woolsack, currently in use by the Lord Chancellor as he presided, was more than enough for her.

It was Julian in whom her interest resided. Julian sat in place and made no contribution to the stupefying debate. His eyes were half-closed. Heather was hoping to be in his company later on, however, and had written him at the Albany to that effect. She had known that he would be attending this important debate, and supposed that the missive had reached its destination too late for him to peruse it.

"Isn't he handsome?" she said, and pointed out the man she intended to marry.

"Most distinguished," said her friend, Clarissa Fitton. If there was the slightest tactful reservation in Clarissa's tone, it didn't come through to Heather.

There was a long speech by some gentleman who looked as if his body had sprung from the head of a flower, and another by a messy-looking man with cheeks padded like those of a variety artist. When the latter had finished, there was a recess. The two young ladies left the Strangers' Gallery and filed into the handsomely decorated Peers' Lobby. Heather smiled at her friend, whose father kept her from going out of an afternoon except with a female. A while had passed since they had seen one another, and a certain amount of talking had to be done.

Reaching the brass gates in the north doorway of the lobby, they encountered the arms of six dynasties of English rulers. Briefly they took time to discuss whether one of these was Stewart or Saxon. The matter remained unresolved as Heather looked out for the sight of Julian. Hypnotized into a state of lethargy by the recent discussion, apparently, he didn't come through the well-lit Peers' Corridor.

The young ladies were startled by the sound of laughter from a female. Heather, turning first, saw that it was an acquaintance, Francesca McKinven, who was looking directly at her and laughing.

Heather approached, ready to ask swiftly what it was about her appearance that could be so amusing to the daughter of an untitled father who was merely engaged in some industrial pursuit. She had long ago convinced herself that not every one of her features was of equal comeliness, but saw nothing in such a determination that would rouse derisive laughter in another.

The attempt proved valueless. Francesca simply turned and started out by the south doorway. Heather called the girl's name once, but Miss McKinven didn't falter. Just before her departure, though, she suddenly looked back, a hand over her mouth to stifle added laughter. Only then did she run off.

Frowning, Heather turned to her friend, who had joined the pursuit. "Why should she take me as a figure of fun?"

Clarissa said soothingly, "No doubt Francesca—I forget her last name as we've met once only—has started to suffer from a disturbance of the senses. Nothing else could explain her behavior."

Heather smiled. Clarissa Fitton could tailor a supposition to fit every mysterious occurrence, which was due in part to her father's having kept her from knowing more of The City and its denizens. The realization made Heather wonder to what extent her friend's idea was incorrect. In these circumstances, however, she put a good face on matters and glanced around the room and over to the Peers' Corridor for any sign of Julian.

As ill-luck would have it, Julian failed to make an appearance.

The Prince Consort, in a dazzling varicolored uniform that he might well have designed himself, looked down at a tall man in uniform being escorted into his presence. Bending only slightly from the horse on which he was mounted, Albert pinned a medal upon this man's heart. As the latter withdrew, the Prince Consort bowed very slightly.

Heather was sitting next to Clarissa Fitton in the huge half-circle of seats erected in Hyde Park to hold thousands of onlookers in spite of the February chill. The young ladies had arrived after the two-hour stop at the Lords, Heather finally deciding that Julian would not leave the chamber. Clarissa, wanting to make an afternoon of this rare occasion away from Sir Samuel's jurisdiction, had suggested observing the ceremony.

"Fourteen men altogether are to be decorated," Clarissa whispered from behind a raised palm. "Each is to gain a pension of ten pounds a year."

"It doesn't seem much," Heather murmured, stirred by recollections of the sights she had observed from Julian's carriage. It was not a habit of thought that would have came to her before that occasion. "My family spends that in four or five days."

Clarissa looked a little surprised at the comparison, but held her tongue. She was reflecting on the Prince as a loyal husband with many children. She considered him wooden, unlike Mr. Ambrose Pennymore, a figurehead in the home but a figure on state occasions.

The ceremony done at last, Albert rode away slowly.

"The Queen's delicate condition prohibits her from making a public appearance on this occasion," said the knowledgeable Clarissa, who had been reading the respectable newspapers as ever.

"Perhaps she is also tired of so many ceremonial occasions," said the somewhat more worldly Heather.

"Oh no!" Clarissa was dismayed at the thought.

"You will be able to ask her when you are presented in Court."

"I don't think I ever will be," Clarissa said regretfully.

Heather looked sympathetic. Clarissa's father, Sir Samuel, was a respectable man with influence in Whig and Tory councils alike. Neither girl could have known that the Royal Family and their staff had recoiled from the prospect of formal presentation by a young woman whose family wealth was earned in so prosaic, not to say undignified, an industry. Royal acknowledgment would have brought true pleasure to Clarissa, but it was not, apparently, to be her portion.

To keep her own mind from dwelling on the disappointment, Clarissa told Heather about the recent brief meeting with Mr. Ambrose Pennymore, adding shyly that she expected to be fortunate enough to see far more of the banker.

"That is truly wonderful," Heather said, decidedly pleased that Mr. Pennymore's affections might be engaged, so to speak, elsewhere. Now that she thought of it, a closeted young lady like Miss Fitton and an unworldly gentleman like Ambrose would get on swimmingly. "I am most happy for you both and will be a bridesmaid at St. George's in Hanover Square upon the happy occasion in future."

Clarissa, of course, blushed. "Matters haven't reached that level."

"With you as a willing participant, Clarissa, they soon will."

"Do you really think so?"

"I am certain of it."

The girls were beaming at one another when there was a sudden snigger from one of the departing members of the audience. Sharply reminded of the recent unseemly demonstration in the Peers' Corridor, Heather turned. A young man she had briefly met at some ball was looking directly at her.

"Have you done much drawing lately?" he asked mockingly. Another young man in his presence chortled at the sally. A third said something quietly to the others, and the three of them walked off.

Heather was almost openmouthed. Other witnesses to the ceremony were clotted too thickly in the area for her to attempt an unseemly pursuit of the three young men.

Clarissa frowned. "Why were two of them laughing?"

"I don't have the foggiest notion," Heather admitted. "Do you suppose it has anything to do with that foolish Francesca back at the Lords?"

"Why would it?"

"When people suddenly behave in so unpleasant a fashion without any apparent complicity and in different times and places, there must be a connection," Heather said firmly. "And why under this sun or any other should he have asked about my drawing?"

"I don't know." Clarissa, of course, had a suggestion based on scant knowledge of another's circumstances. "When you arrive home, consult with your family."

"My brother, perhaps." Heather didn't want Mamma making all sorts of speculations that put a daughter in the light of someone who had committed at least a solitary social transgression. "I think we may now return to our homes in a leisurely fashion."

"I will drop you off at Brook Street, first," Clarissa said, wanting to lengthen the time spent away from her own house. "The carriage will take me back afterward."

That suggested route was impractical, as Clarissa must have realized, too. Accepting the reason for her choice, however, Heather nodded.

"Certainly, sister," she said, using a term of affection that was rare with her. "Let us proceed straightaway."

As soon as Heather stepped into the large sitting room downstairs in Brook Street, Maurice said something in the way of an excuse and hurried up to his studio, as he often called that aerie in the attic.

Mamma, despite her russet swallowtail dress, looked pale. She asked anxiously, "You are not planning to do anything after supper, Heather, I hope? Good. Then we must have some speech together at that time."

Even in the eternally optimistic tones of her mother it was discernible that she felt Heather would only be prepared, after a substantial repast, to grapple with whatever the bad news might be.

"I would like to know," Heather began.

It was in vain. Mamma, briskly saying that the cook's work needed constant supervision, strode off.

Turning to go up to her own room, Heather saw Beryl in the hallway. The maid was briskly rearranging the dust on one of those oriental-inspired monstrosities with which Mamma had inflicted the household. Heather's eyes were avoided. When Beryl became aware of being examined, she looked around long enough to offer a hesi-

tant smile and then turned back in palpable relief. It was impossible
to avoid the conclusion that Beryl, too, knew the worst.

"Please come upstairs with me now," Heather said politely.

"Miss, I was instructed to give the furniture a dusting!"

"I have need of your services," Heather snapped. This was approximately true.

Beryl, the dustcloth in one hand as a badge of office, followed
upstairs.

Heather didn't speak before she had walked across the red carpet
of her room and sat down at the polished mahogany desk to take off
the four-button shoes from Dawson's in the Burlington Arcade,
shoes that constricted the bones of her feet. Mamma had insisted
more than once that the shoe-type was healthier for a young girl
than laces, and Heather occasionally wore these if she thought she
would be away from Brook Street for only a short time. She hadn't
expected a protracted sojourn on this day.

Confronted by the maid's unease, it was only humane to make
the discussion between them as brief as possible. Heather didn't
happen to be a hard-shelled Londoner who accepted the knowledge
that certain subjects of discussion were frowned upon between mistress and servant.

"Do you know anything about my affairs that I should know,
too?"

"Miss?"

Was it Heather's imagination, or had the maid flinched?

"I believe you heard the question."

"Miss, what do you think I could know?" Beryl's voice had risen
and she was looking around like some trapped animal.

"I can't say." Heather considered. "Whatever this social *gaffe* of
mine might be, it is known to people with whom I am only slightly
acquainted. I will myself be apprised of the details shortly, but
would appreciate your transmitting them to me at this time."

"Yes, Miss 'eather." It seemed that the thought of the young
mistress's appreciation was enough to move Beryl. "I—I don't know
personal-like, you understand. I've 'eard about it."

"Beryl, it is admitted far and wide that I am a patient female, but

I can assure you that I am fully capable of screaming until the roof falls in."

It wasn't true about Heather's lack of control, as mistress and servant both knew. The maid couldn't help smiling at that image.

"Yes, miss, everybody is afraid of your awful temper."

"Be that as it may," Heather said, subduing her own smile of acknowledgment because of the very real irritation she was experiencing, "this shilly-shally accomplishes nothing."

"No, miss."

It occurred to Heather that Julian would have been amused at her insistence on directness, as it was exactly the opposite of what she desired, though for entirely different reasons, at the beginning of her dealings with him.

"Miss, as you demands it, I will tell you what I 'ave 'eard. Do you know the penny sheet called *Society Deeds?*"

Heather was surprised. The reference was to a six-page newspaper that printed bulletins about sports along with gossip of fashionable figures. The first page generally showed some odious male in full fig and busily leering at an attractive woman who was more than interested in his attentions. Heather and a few friends had occasionally chortled over the publication's excesses, but she didn't think she had seen its inside as many as three times.

"Have they printed my name?"

"I—yes, miss."

Heather was tempted to throw back her head and laugh. "No doubt they've been saying that I am stealing away into some arboreal dell with Lord Palmerston himself."

Beryl ought to have smiled at the conception of a comely young woman finding romance with the Queen's elderly First Minister. No smile appeared, however.

"What *have* they been saying?"

"Well, Miss 'eather, like I tells you I 'aven't seen every word of it, that I 'aven't."

"You are avoiding the question," Heather said, with all the severity of which she was capable. "Please tell me in so many words what has been suggested about me."

"It's not anything they've—" Beryl began, then looked down unhappily. "It's—it's what they show."

"What *could* you mean?" Heather considered rising to put both hands around the maid's long neck and shake her like dice in a box. Such an extreme of behavior was entirely beyond her capacities, however. "Please tell me this minute exactly what you mean."

"There is a picture, miss." Beryl's voice was choked by reluctance to speak.

Remembering that dolt in Hyde Park who had somehow managed to make the idea of drawing sound lascivious—now that she considered it again, his intent must have been exactly in that direction—Heather waited to hear what else there was to be said. She trusted in silence to bring forth the maid's knowledge, and her trust was not incorrectly placed.

"There is a picture of Mr. Pennymore in it, a picture in black pencil. The face looks exaggerated."

"How can this involve me?" Surprised as she was, Heather had entirely forgotten the answer she ought to have known by this time.

It was offered unmistakably, now. "The—the thing shows Mr. Pennymore as a baby."

Heather, her mouth open, closed it abruptly. Like Norman Gateshead not long ago, she experienced the distinctly unpleasant sensation of reeling in place.

"Your signature is on it," Beryl added, needlessly.

"I vividly recall that particular screed," Heather had to admit, finally trusting herself to speak. "Why should it be considered wicked?"

"Oh, it's—well, Miss 'eather, they print only the face and that part with your signature on it. The editor writes that 'e can't print what else there is of the sketch of a person without—pardon me, Miss 'eather—without a stitch."

For the first time, Heather fully understood the implications of what had taken place. Some epigrammatist with a talent for understatement could describe the event as a calamity.

"But everyone will think that I drew the entire—that is, all of Ambrose from the front."

"Yes, miss." Beryl nodded unhappily, a tendril of dark hair being set free from her cap and thereby adding to the emphasis. "The editor of *Society Deeds* writes that the entire sketch can be viewed in his office by qualified authorities."

Heather was too dazed to wonder who might constitute the latter. It crossed her mind that if Tessie O'Loughrane's consistent reading of novels had caused so much difficulty for her in The City, then Heather's own lapse might result in her being skewered, socially speaking.

"I drew lines for a cherub's legs and nothing more."

"Yes, miss, I kn— Yes, miss."

No added information of worth was going to be gleaned from this source.

"Thank you, Beryl. You may resume your duties now."

The maid ventured a commiserating smile and then made a swift departure.

Left alone, Heather was well aware that it was the maid who must have released that infernal sketch from the precincts of the Shaw demesne. It posed a difficulty with which she, or Mamma, would have to deal in time. The impossibility of reposing trust in someone capable of such an action was on her mind as she addressed herself to the next item on her self-imposed agenda.

This consisted of a note to be written to Mr. Ambrose Pennymore. Taking pen in hand by its pink holder, she indited the missive swiftly from a full heart. She said that she was not responsible for the public knowledge of what had been intended as an affectionate gesture, then added that she had spent much of the day with Miss Fitton and that the latter thought well of him.

Although she enclosed her best wishes and meant them, it was beyond Heather's powers to avoid feeling a little like some public hangman extending sympathies to the family of a victim.

Standing in front of the upright piano at the southeast end of the large sitting room in Brook Street, Mrs. Shaw paused and lifted a dragon candlestick holder. Patiently she eased her free hand against the Arab scarf that lined the piano ledge, touching it for dust. A forefinger soon raced around the lower circle of the porcelain vase lifted from the colorful runner, briefly disturbing the six-colored

Japanese fan that had been positioned nearby. Having spent her early years in genteel poverty, it seemed to Heather that Mamma had celebrated Maurice Shaw's surge of income by taking on all the airs and graces of the Fashionables as imagined by a flower girl in the twopenny stalls at the Alhambra. Unkind though the conception may have been, at moments like this Heather found it irresistible.

"Has any correspondence arrived for me?" she asked.

She had dressed for supper in her oversized violet French chip, which had the effect of taking attention from whatever feature seemed weakest to her at a given time. In addition, she had put on laced shoes. There was some tendency for her face to flush unbecomingly when anyone looked at her since the recent revelation, but she supposed that such a habit wouldn't last long.

"If there is anything of that nature for you, it is on the hall table," Mamma said, looking up compassionately at her daughter.

Heather, now aware of the reason behind that particular attitude, said quietly, "I know about the day's issue of *Society Deeds.*"

Mamma put in promptly, "There is nothing to cause you even the slightest worry, Heather."

Maurice, who had appeared behind his sister, suddenly snorted.

Mamma said pointedly, "Maurice, dear, I will accept no saddening speeches just before supper. Or at the table, for that matter."

"Or at any other time," Maurice said moodily, enunciating his sister's sudden thought along with his own.

Heather found a bare table in the hall. No correspondence had been delivered for her. A letter from Julian in response to hers of the morning would have been only natural. It crossed her mind for the first time that the Marquis of Thetford had possibly been too upset about the incident as recorded on the pages of *Society Deeds* to seek her out at the Peers Lobby.

Such an interpretation seemed unlikely from Julian, who knew his mind if anyone did. Nonetheless, facts had to be faced. She had heard nothing from him, perhaps because of business at the Lords but more likely because he was shamed to consider himself in propinquity with someone of so notorious a reputation.

Still doubtful of his *volte-face* and telling herself repeatedly that the difficulty would eventually be clarified, Heather returned to the large sitting room. She was in time to see Beryl manifest herself at the door and curtsy.

"Supper is served," the maid intoned.

"Thank you," said Mamma with a steely heartiness.

It was a tone that Heather recognized. Clearly Mamma had accepted the knowledge that Beryl was the one who had betrayed the family's interest.

The dilemma posed by such behavior was one that even the everhopeful Delphine Shaw was cognizant of. Only Beryl and a cook had been serving them for many months, and to send Beryl away would leave the family bereft of domestic help outside the kitchen. Momentarily also dismissing the new problem from her thoughts, Mamma took Maurice's arm and led the way into the dining room.

Heather, her mind a million miles away from even the most pressing of household difficulties, followed.

CHAPTER TWELVE

Scandal Finds Ambrose Pennymore

If a lack of correspondence was disturbing to Heather, it can be said that a plethora of missives was equally disturbing to Mr. Ambrose Pennymore.

Having returned to the vicinity of Garrick Street at nightfall, he was initially tired. He had passed a typically full day at the Pennymore Bank, leaving his father behind to transact some business no one else from the bank could manage so satisfactorily from the senior Pennymore's point of view. Ambrose now found himself facing Gateshead bearing a salver with three letters.

"Two of these must have been returned," he said needlessly, a hollow feeling in the pit of his stomach.

"I fear so, sir," the butler agreed. "Two were brought back by a messenger."

These letters had been written to Clarissa, as he now felt emboldened to think of that lovely creature. One letter would have sufficed, but he had declined to halt the muse in a second flight and had inscribed another after a brief pause. Nonetheless they had been returned, presumably unread.

It seemed like the fitting end to a day in which people he hardly knew had unsettled him by suddenly covering their lips to smile as soon as he came in sight, or turned away to laugh heartily. The possibility loomed that numerous inhabitants of The City were a little disturbed in the midst of a long winter.

He felt no inclination to examine the third note, which had been sent by Heather Shaw. Ambrose's conscience bothered him about Miss Shaw, to whom he had offered much attention before turning away when the delightful and competent Clarissa Fitton entered his life.

Only one course of action seemed open to him. A trip to Bennet Street would be desirable. There he could learn from Miss Fitton's own dear lips the reasons for her behavior.

Ambrose dressed himself in funereal black, with a white shirt and loosely knotted string tie. He wished he had acquired somewhere the shrewdness of any costermonger. In dealing with a female, the son of Leslie Pennymore always felt himself at a severe disadvantage.

"This one matter must be settled tonight," he told his reflection in the mirror, which seemed in perfect agreement.

Disdaining the services of a hansom cab, Ambrose walked past Bedford Row and the houses with elaborate fretwork from entrance to gable peak. The night was so chill that he felt badly dressed in spite of a dark wool cape, and he was sure that a winter pea-souper was on the way. In that sort of fog the wind seemed to lie doggo and every passing edifice was burdened with a gray-and-white ring. Unknown young females walking by themselves on the street would suddenly burst into inexplicable giggles. It was the sort of climate that a Londoner accepted as his portion on this plane of existence, entitling him to a happy afterlife for having endured it.

At Bennet Street the door was answered by the saturnine Fitton butler, whose lips quirked at sight of him just as had happened on the previous day.

"Would Miss Fitton be expecting you, sir?" asked Turnbull as if he knew the answer himself.

"I'm afraid not."

The butler considered the problem posed by Ambrose Pennymore's existence. "Please come in, sir," he said at last, making the best of this matter.

His cape wasn't taken, which signified that Turnbull didn't anticipate that the visitor would make a burdensome stay. Somberly Ambrose was escorted into the large sitting room, with its surprising lack of clutter. He didn't know that Miss Fitton preferred spaciousness in rooms, and had triumphantly overruled Sir Samuel in this, as in so many minor matters.

From another part of the establishment there issued a sound like some animal in the throes of indignation. Ambrose felt that instead of a discussion with Clarissa he would be conferring directly with the earth-closet mogul.

His intuition proved to have been accurate. Sir Samuel himself, proceeded by a light brown bulldog almost as large as Maurice Shaw, surged into the room. Sir Samuel's eyes seemed flinty. The man who had overruled all opposition so as to introduce a new model of convenience with a one-pound pull rather than the traditional pound-and-a-half, was in no mood to stand for the visit of someone he obviously now considered an undesirable.

"Are you here on business?" Sir Samuel inquired through gritted teeth, not the clearest form of communication. The glow from mirrored candles cast a satanic gleam upon his bald head as well as eyebrows that suddenly resembled spikes.

"Not at all, sir." Ambrose, as was only to be expected, spoke politely. "Indeed, I asked to see Miss Fitton."

"And why did you do that?"

The knight's sharp tone caused Ambrose to draw himself up a little more firmly in polite opposition.

"Surely, sir, this could be discussed more sensibly with Miss Fitton herself."

Sir Samuel, however, seemed indisposed to wait much longer for clarification of the question he had posed in so hostile a manner. A growl issued either from his throat or the bulldog's. This latter's temper seemed frayed as well.

"I would like Miss Fitton to apprise me of her reason for returning my letters."

"It is of no importance to you, but I can say that my daughter didn't return anything."

"You—*you* took it on yourself to send back the letters I had written her?"

"Indubitably."

"Might I point out, sir, that the letters were not addressed to you?"

"I noticed that," Sir Samuel agreed with heavy jocosity that suited him. "As soon as I saw the odious things defacing my hall table, it dawned on me that they were addressed to someone else."

"And you returned them without informing Miss Fitton?" In one way Ambrose felt better, in another he couldn't help feeling infinitely worse.

"That's correct, too," Sir Samuel snapped, almost as if he was once again arguing the advantages of a one-pound pull. "I see all of my daughter's correspondence before she does."

Ambrose sensed that it was no time for him to remark that Clarissa Fitton shouldn't be completely sheltered from the young man who had so suddenly and irrevocably fallen in love with her. Because he was possessed of intelligence, he ignored the opportunity to make further comment along lines that wouldn't be considered tactful.

"It wasn't the contents of my letters which caused your disapproval," Ambrose pointed out, stirred to a fresh burst of speech by the other's inexplicable opposition. "Those letters hadn't been opened."

"I disapproved of the sender," Sir Samuel said pointedly, further clarifying a matter that wasn't in great doubt by this time. "I still do."

Ambrose blinked in understandable confusion. He wasn't able to accustom himself to the change of attitude on the part of this titan of industry. At the first meeting between himself and Clarissa, not two days ago, Sir Samuel had been approving in the extreme. Now it was almost as if Father Christmas had thought better of warmth and kindness, then transformed himself into an ogre.

"I would like to know what has occasioned this unsettling change of heart."

"So you claim to be ignorant of recent events." Either the mogul or his bulldog was breathing deeply. "You mean to persuade me that you haven't looked at a certain penny sheet today, I presume. Do you claim that no one has pointed out the object to you or that you fail to understand its varied and hideous implications?"

Ambrose was uncertain how to reply. Every word of this elder's jeremiad was crystal clear, but added together they didn't make the least sense.

At this juncture, Sir Samuel drew himself up and raised a finger in the direction of the nearest door. His manner indicated that he had been civil long enough, and now it was time to be more direct.

"I order you to leave," he said. "If you never again deface so much as the shadow of my threshold, your absence will be deeply appreciated. Not to evade my meaning, Pennymore, I long to see the last of you in my home."

The bulldog, snuffling deep in its throat, was expressing like sentiments as best it could.

Ambrose spared a cautious glance for the beast, who certainly refrained from violating the *code duello* by engaging in battle on his own grounds.

"Very well," the banker said, careful not to raise his voice loud enough to offend the four-legged auditor. "Because of your advanced age, Sir Samuel, I am leaving now."

"When we have any business to transact in the future, I shall meet with you at your father's emporium," Sir Samuel said. "In that way, you will not again be able to corrupt any young woman of even my slightest acquaintance."

Ambrose hardly heard the last robust sentiments. If they had penetrated the haze of anger and dismay in which he found himself, they would have been as inexplicable to him as everything else that had happened to him since nightfall.

The sorely perplexed young man decided against walking back toward Garrick Street. He wasn't particularly hungry for the company of his family. Impelled by furies which had manifested themselves for this occasion, he determined to look in at a gambling hell.

Such behavior was unheard of on Ambrose's part before a working day. Nor could he by any stretch of imagination be considered an *habitué* of such establishments. He had visited on an occasion or two, generally in the company of friends who were experienced at this type of endeavor. A game of faro had once caught his interest, mainly because it would have been impossible for the establishment to cheat in its own favor and thereby determine the outcome. Nonetheless he had been divested of six pounds and several guineas by the playing. As an investment, it seemed to him entirely beneath contempt.

Relegating his strictures to one side, however briefly, he was determined to make some effort at subduing his recent agonizing sorrows. Words like "implications" and "penny sheets" seemed permanently lodged in his mind, sentiments as spoken in Sir Samuel's grating accents. Little wonder, then, that Ambrose Pennymore found it impossible to walk without his fists knotted in helpless anger. After his second street accident, in which he cannoned into a portly gentleman proceeding homeward, Ambrose took a hansom. In this vehicle he discovered that it was momentarily impossible for him to sit in one place.

The only gambling hell he could recall by name was that of Ballauf's on Mount Street, and it was there that the hansom proceeded on his instructions. Passing the orderly who watched for guardians of the law, he deposited his cape with a young man in an alcove and hurried up a set of dingy stairs.

A rise in the threshold, over which Ambrose nearly fell, defeated his intention of striding into the place as if he owned it. He was in the supplementary room, given over to rest, of a sort, where guests stood or sat and ate or drank as they wished. Behind a thick door at the far end, lay the virtual *oubliette* that was dedicated to the art and craft of losing one's money.

A dark-haired girl who had been bantering with a drunk suddenly looked up and saw him. She was possessed of the exceptionally white skin associated by most men with Irish milkmaids. Ambrose was certain he had never seen this young lady, but her eyes narrowed as she was obviously trying to recall a memory of him.

"Don't I know you?" The girl's tones were a Londoner's, but not quite *pukka* by Ambrose's high standards. "Did you used to be Meg Davisson's favorite gentleman friend?"

"No, I did not." Ambrose affixed a smile as he denied anything in common with this creature. He did know an elderly Duke of that name who borrowed from Pennymore's Bank, but hoped that there wasn't any relationship between the peer and that dissolute Meg, whoever she might be. "Pardon me."

"But I *know* you," the girl insisted, and turned to another. "Don't you know this one?"

The second, a thin girl with her hair tinted white, smiled in a way that reminded Ambrose unmistakably of other smiles from men and women during the last day. It was as if each was informing him that he or she knew his best-kept secret. Not being so fortunate as to have any secrets of a shocking nature, Ambrose was always taken aback. It was a difficulty he felt determined to resolve in dealing with these two representatives of London social strata.

"Who *doesn't* know him except you?" asked the second girl, chuckling.

An unbelieving young banker suddenly felt his shoulders circled by that girl's arm. With her other hand, she twisted some of the buttons of his jacket, popping one of them. Her hands felt warm, but their proximity was disturbing in light of the unsolved mystery.

"Now look here!" Ambrose sat down forcefully, legs crossed and shoulders hunched so that neither girl would be tempted into another show of affection. "I don't know you ladies and I'm sure that neither of you knows me."

Taking that as an invitation for further talk, the second girl approached. A wide smile showed the regular teeth that she must have realized were her very best feature.

"I've certainly seen you!" She was sniggering now.

"You must tell me where that happened."

The blonde said, "Stay on," and spoke to a man nearby. This one directed her to a waiter. The latter excused himself briefly and returned with a penny sheet in hand. Ambrose, remembering Sir Samuel's recent barbed reference to such instruments of communication, felt his senses quickening with anticipation.

And in another moment he knew full well why everything in his life had suddenly gone wrong.

It was clear from the fragments of illustration in *Society Deeds* that he had been caricatured as a baby and without clothes, that every reader would think of certain parts of his anatomy as having been limned and exaggerated as well. He would be considered little better than a rake, a trifler with women's hearts. Presumably all of London was now convinced that he and Heather Shaw were partnered in an illicit affair.

And in that moment's illumination, Ambrose knew, too, that the note from Heather which had been delivered to him must contain some apology for what had taken place.

Not that it mattered now. To Ambrose's mind it was impossible for him ever to regain the admiration of Clarissa Fitton or the tolerance of her Argus-eyed father. Without intending it for a moment, Heather Shaw had destroyed his life.

Nor could he forget the disaster for even a moment. He wasn't blessed with a head for consecutive doses of spirits that could have offered unconsciousness. Such immoderate refreshment only made him ill. He considered gambling a waste of time and intelligence. As for romping with the two fair creatures in front of him, their only interest in Ambrose Pennymore was in the sudden celebrity he loathed. His interest in them was therefore less than nil.

It was a night, in sum, when no mode of relaxation whatever would present itself.

Ambrose, blessed with practicality, made the best of it. He returned toward Garrick Street. Deftly avoiding both parents, he went up to his room and bed. Here he attempted to gain a night's repose he had so richly earned by his day's endeavors, but was only fitfully successful.

CHAPTER THIRTEEN

Fatal Embarrassment

"I have not heard from Ambrose," said Miss Clarissa Fitton, interrupting the silent reading of *Barchester Towers* as her esteemed male
progenitor came into the upstairs sitting room and left the door
wide open. "That is why I am unhappy."

"Umf," said Sir Samuel, who had unwisely put the question.

"I have gone so far as to write him and indicate that I would not
frown at his further attentions, if he should by any chance be unsure
on that point."

Leave it to Clarissa to attempt taking matters into her own hands,
thought the restless knight who had fathered her.

"However he has made no response," Clarissa added.

Knowing perfectly well that his daughter's correspondence to that
foul young man had never left Bennet Street, Sir Samuel was hardly
surprised by this confidence.

"Umf," the knight said once more. His recent path had diverged
from that of the family bulldog, Dizzy by name, or the animal would
otherwise have proffered a similar observation.

"I hoped that Ambrose might have just called," Clarissa said, not
having to add that she had heard the front door open and close a
few moments ago. "Apparently I was in error."

Sir Samuel decided, as often before in life, that it was preferable
to be cruel in order to be kind.

"You will never see or hear from him again, Clarissa, if I have my
way, and I intend to do so."

"Pardon me?" His daughter could hardly believe her ears, an
uncommon occurrence in that young lady's life.

Sir Samuel repeated his statement only with more *brio* on the word "never." The late David Garrick, could he have been among the present company, would have nodded in approval at Sir Samuel's reading of that line.

"But I must see Ambrose again!"

"If that event happens, my dear, your balance will be somewhat impeded because of standing over my dead body," said Sir Samuel, with an urbanity that many of his business colleagues would have considered was beyond his capacities. "In no other way will you see or speak to that fiend."

It has been indicated previously during the course of this tale that its personnel responded differently to the news that their worlds appeared to have come to an end. Norman Gateshead, as we have seen, had felt despair. The fright experienced by Beryl Olton has been evoked with terrifying precision. Nor has Heather's shock been gainsaid, to say nothing of Ambrose's feeling that had been unkindly eviscerated. Much space has been given to these varied *longueurs,* to the *sturm* as well as the *drang.*

With Clarissa, however, a different response is encountered. Instead of feeling like a chicken *soubise* just removed from a scalding oven, Clarissa Fitton sat up straight, then tossed her blond hair defiantly and glowered.

"I want to know why you have made this decision for me," she insisted.

"Why? Because the young man is a Mephistopheles, a Moloch, a Belial!"

"Tell me the details of his offense before I accept your decision."

Sir Samuel longed for the days when a daughter gave unquestioning obedience to the fiats of a loving father. Except for a muffled oath and the striking of a fist into an opened palm, he gave no indication whatever of his strong feelings.

"I cannot tell you the salacious details," he insisted.

" 'Salacious details' involving Ambrose? Now I *must* be apprised of this development!"

The knight supposed that sooner or later a female friend (he couldn't believe that the news wasn't available over the length and breadth of The City, from Belgravia to the depths of Limehouse) would inform Clarissa of the facts anent the vile Ambrose. He decided to tell Clarissa himself and cushion the shock to her delicate system.

"But it doesn't mean that Ambrose was sketched entirely," Clarissa began, as soon as she had absorbed the details in spite of her father's hesitations.

"It doesn't mean anything else," Sir Samuel insisted stoutly.

"I disagree. Further, the mere existence of some drawing doesn't mean that Ambrose has carried on with Heather Shaw. Indeed, I will venture to say that nothing of the sort whatever has happened between those two."

"Such indecency takes place among the most unexpected participants," Sir Samuel said, and then cleared his throat hastily. "So, at least, I have been given to understand."

"Can you not ask Ambrose for the truth?"

"The truth is plain, Clarissa, perfectly plain. Ambrose Pennymore posed for that sketch at a time when he was wholly undraped and in the young woman's presence."

Clarissa performed a motion that in a woman of the lower classes would have been called writhing. Certainly she was exploring areas of unhappiness that were new to her.

"Is it not possible to find mitigating circumstances in his behavior?" she asked.

While shaking his head, Sir Samuel silently swore at females with their infernal suggestions! Clarissa's mother had been exactly the same way.

"If I should see Ambrose at all, certainly I will do the polite thing and offer a greeting." Clarissa's lips closed mulishly, indicating that she planned on offering far more personal a public response to him as well.

"Any ball to which Pennymore is invited," Sir Samuel insisted, "is one which you will not attend."

Clarissa drew both hands up to her head as if to keep the latter in place. "I have never been so importunate in the past, Father, but I ask you to consider in this case if some *modus vivendi* is possible."

Sir Samuel silently damned the concept of even the most rudimentary education for a woman when the male with whom she dealt was not fluent in whatever language she may have been spouting.

"You will never see him again," Sir Samuel insisted doggedly, arms extended as if to take in a whole world fully occupied but bare of Ambrose Pennymore. "It is bad enough that I have to deal with him in the way of commerce."

He turned to leave. It was true, as he indicated, that he needed money to advertise and issue a new model of the convenience, as he most often thought of it, with painted flowers on the sides. Added expenses would be involved in doing so, and the Pennymore Bank had always been a sensible dealer of the needful.

It had occurred to Sir Samuel, too, that his attempt to beautify the convenience might find favor for him when new titles were conferred. He would have given much to be styled as Sir Samuel Fitton, Bart.

"But, Father," Clarissa persisted, "I have become deeply interested in Ambrose despite our brief acquaintance, and I want to see him again so as to determine the extent of my feelings and his. It is not a matter of merely flirting."

Sir Samuel doubted if his daughter had ever engaged in a protracted flirtation, and found himself considering her indulgence of that type with powerful repugnance which he supposed was wrong. But there was no law in any statute books and no custom whatever insisting that his daughter had to marry a fiend. Such an activity would be carrying a suitable idea much too far.

"No," said the knight firmly, pausing by the door but speaking so quietly that none of the domestic staff could hear his animadversions on the subject. "I am now going to the stables, where I can have a horsewhip sequestered for possible use upon the person of that accursed young Pennymore if he ever so much as approaches you again."

"Pappa," Clarissa protested, distress causing her to utilize a form of speech she hadn't favored since childhood.

"Should I have occasion to employ that particular implement," Sir Samuel continued, with a wholly unbecoming relish, "I will have it destroyed afterward, as I wouldn't then want it touching a flank of any horse of mine."

Clarissa fell silent. The point had been made unmistakably clear that Sir Samuel felt an extreme antipathy toward dear Ambrose, as Clarissa rebelliously thought of him. There remained nothing further to be said at this time.

On his way to the hall table for that morning's correspondence, Maurice Shaw looked around him with a moment's satisfaction. He had campaigned for months to obtain his mother's permission to install gas lighting rather than continuing to use hanging lamps in every room and paraffin with glass chimneys over burning wicks so as to concentrate the brightness. Candlesticks of tallow had previously been placed on flat dishes for employment by those of the family, nearly always himself, who returned late at night.

"There are gas fixtures in the palace," he had said by way of opening the subject to discussion one night.

No argument proved necessary after that. Maurice had spent his free time for the next several weeks in consultation with a minor functionary from the Ministry of Public Works. This latter finally pointed out that the attic wasn't fireproof and that escaped gas might collect in ceiling spaces. As for using gas fixtures in the attic, the Works man virtually crossed himself against evil at the very notion. For the two major floors, however, hanging lamps, gas mantels, and gasoliers would be appropriate.

The installation caused some interest and apprehension from neighbors, but Maurice accepted the risks in the name of progress and left it to his mother and sister to pacify them. By the time that chore was undertaken and completed he had involved himself in the choice of new household tools, from carpet sweeper to knife sharpener and mechanical dish lift. He had inspected these pieces before purchase with enormous relish for the machinery's careful construction.

As a result of all that meddling he was able to walk across a spotless floor to the hall table on this morning and clearly read two letters addressed to him and dispensing with his services as a portraitist.

Sir Evelyn Mark, possibly the last knight-banneret in the Empire, had written a wholly uncivil note accusing Maurice of being a sub-

verter of young women who taught them wicked crafts—whatever
those might be.

The second note, from the Earl of Fearguise, contained regrets
and a small check for Maurice's efforts to this date. The Earl's
family had probably insisted on the severance. The presence of the
stipend was unsurprising. Irish peers had a strong tendency to com-
miserate with those who have fallen, whether through any fault of
their own or, as in Maurice's case, not.

"Have you received bad news, dear?"

It was Mamma, passing from the kitchen to the stairway that
would take her upward, most likely to speak to Heather. His sister
had closeted herself since perceiving the illustration in a copy of
Society Deeds. Heather wasn't in a bad temper, and happened not
to be the sort who cried, fortunately, or tears would have been heard
up and down Brook Street. Indeed she had remarked only that the
caricature was well reproduced in the penny sheet and staunchly
refused to say anything more about the subject. But she had also
refused to leave her room, causing Mrs. Shaw some unhappiness.

Maurice, noting only that his mother's costume was an ill match
for her coloring, summoned up a smile.

"Irritating news, Mamma, but not of major importance," he said,
tampering with the truth. "A couple of subjects will not be able to
keep their next appointments."

"An onset of collective illness, I expect," said Delphine Shaw
shrewdly, with understandable anger toward the recalcitrant sitters.
"Cases of fatal embarrassment, possibly."

Maurice nodded almost before he could stop himself. Dissembling was largely foreign to his nature, and this attempt at mini-
mizing the family difficulty had been addressed and executed with
the greatest circumspection.

"Of course you think there will be more who shirk their duty as
clients," Mamma said. "Do we have the wherewithal to survive a
period of drought, so to speak?"

Maurice shrugged. He had gambled heavily during two years in
London. The family coffers were by no means empty, but only a
brief drought, in Mamma's word, would be required before danger
signals became audible.

"It might be possible to establish ourselves in Edinburgh," he said. "Perhaps that is where we should have gone in the first place."

"No," Mamma insisted, her light brows dropping so determinedly that Maurice wondered yet again why he had been unable to paint them successfully in attempting a portrait of her. "We Scots pay for necessities only when the procurator fiscal is at the door, and for luxuries hardly at all."

He smiled. Mamma generally took a certain pride in examples of Scots prudence with money. Her own ancestry never interfered with the pleasure of telling some apocryphal anecdote in which a countryman of theirs had got the better of an aristocratic Briton. At this time, though, she was entirely serious.

"Furthermore, I want to see your sister settled with Julian, the Marquis of Thetford."

To Maurice, such an outcome now seemed unlikely. Heather had confided with rue that the Marquis hadn't appeared at yesterday's session of Parliament to see her waiting for him in the Peers Lobby. It seemed indicative of the man's feelings. Always ready to think the worst and ascribe it to realism, Maurice envisaged a sour future for his sister, a worthless one for himself, and a frantic one for his mother presiding over the family's decay.

There was the sound of knocking at the door. Beryl, moving swiftly and avoiding others' eyes as she was doing these days, made haste to answer. The door was opened on a wedge of sunlight that would have been useful to Maurice if he had been painting. In the sun, in dark bowler and darker cutaway, tight trousers and ankle-boots, stood Julian Wyse, the Marquis of Thetford.

CHAPTER FOURTEEN

A Visit Is Held in Abeyance

Heather had immured herself in her room so as to be apprised immediately in case there was a note from Julian. It was an explanation that Maurice wouldn't have credited, although Mamma knew the truth without a word on the subject having been exchanged between the two females.

Heather was not entirely astonished, therefore, when Mamma invaded the premises *sans* even a preliminary tap against the door.

"You must come down," Mamma said immediately, her eyes round in pleasure and awe. "*He* is here."

It was the work of a moment for Heather to open her mouth wide in pleased surprise, then turn to the mirror. Having decided that the high-necked lavender day dress gave her cheeks virtually an Ambrose Pennymore effect of disconcerting prominence, and knowing full well that whatever apparel she chose would present some defect to her skeptical eyes, she simply looked away.

"Has he told you why he wants to see me?"

"There is no need for that," Mrs. Shaw said enthusiastically. "He wants to express his support for you in this time of travail."

Heather would anticipate no happy outcome until it materialized, presumably with help from herself or Julian.

"Perhaps," she said, and wondered if the hope was clear in her voice.

It must have been. Mamma unexpectedly placed herself between Heather and the door, and for a brief time Heather wondered if Mamma wasn't going to descend before her and speak to Julian, thereby cushioning the effect, as she might conceive it, of any bad news.

"Listen to me, child," Mamma said firmly. "He has come to one of the least popular establishments in all of fashionable London on this day, and he has done it because of your presence here. He cares for you, and I know you well enough to realize that you feel the same way for him."

Heather nodded, not at all shy about acknowledging that her heart had been captured by a denizen of Norfolk.

Mamma made a sudden sound from between her lips, connoting petulance. "I confess it surpasses my understanding to know why a female and male can look at each other and have only a few brief conversations, whereupon they decide upon being mated once and forever. Perhaps my own age and experience of the world have betrayed me. Nonetheless, I feel that such behavior is un-Scottish and un-British as well. However, fascinating as that speculative path happens to be, it is not entirely to the point."

Heather gestured her impatience to meet Julian yet again.

"In a moment," said Mrs. Shaw. "I want you to descend, to listen to what he has to say, and to make nothing of his having been unavailable to you during yesterday's proceedings at the Lords. There might have been reasons you don't know. Don't be a coquette with him, Heather, and dinna fash' yersel'," she added, reverting briefly to a Scottish expression as proof of her concern. "Be an understanding friend. I realize that the course I indicate would be your first impulse under other circumstances, knowing you as well as I do. What I ask is that you follow your first impulse."

Heather found herself strongly moved. Mamma had assumed that her daughter was unaware of how to respond with a full heart to the first man she loved. She was being protected, not for the first time in her experience, to a greater extent than necessary. The attitude that had often enough caused Heather to sink into despair had been clearly invoked for Heather's own good and not that of an older woman determined to show any need for dominating a nubile daughter.

"Dear Mamma," said Heather, to her own surprise, and suddenly kissed Delphine Shaw on a cheek that seemed more fragile to the touch then Heather had remembered.

Before leaving the room, Heather spared another look at herself in the mirror. This time it seemed that the high-necked day dress showed her off to good if not perfect advantage.

Julian spoke briefly with Maurice Shaw. The latter, noticing that Julian's eyes roamed to the front stairs in expectation of Heather's entrance, spoke only a few words in his turn and then left this hive of pseudo-oriental gewgaws. Julian heard the painter's steps ascending heavenward by another wooden path.

Somewhere on the second level and out of Julian's sight, a door opened. A woman's steps could be detected without an excess of effort. It was Heather who descended swiftly rather than pretending that speed wasn't desired by either of them.

In unspoken agreement he embraced her. Heather rested her head on his chest only briefly and then looked up. Her eyes gleamed happily.

She disconnected herself from Julian with some difficulty and led him into the large sitting room. The door was kept open. Here, in the clutter of furnishings that impeded progress for almost every step of the way, it would be possible for them to speak.

Julian made his way through the labyrinth to a Tavistock chair and stood before it rather than be seated.

"I wasn't aware until last night when I read your note, Heather, that you had come down to the Lords to see me," he began, flushing at the omission unavoidable though it had presumably been. "Nor was I able to get away from the floor, as the bill in question would have some effect on the Trades Union movement and I wanted it to be read out with the least possible alteration."

She wasn't surprised by this now, recalling the powerful feelings evoked in him by the plight of poor folk during that sketching trip of theirs into Bermondsey and its environs. It seemed that Mamma's strictures against inappropriate coyness had been of no use. To her way of thinking, any discussion of this matter was now satisfactorily concluded.

"Nor did I write to you last night when I learned of the—the

misunderstanding in some penny sheet," he added, "for the reason
that I planned to see you on this morning."

That point, too, was now satisfactorily interred.

With so much already understood between them, he brought up
another issue for the first time.

"Heather, I have come to feel strongly that you must pay a visit
over the next weekend to my home in Thetford."

Heather's jaw dropped in astonishment that was not at all
feigned. She was more surprised, although she had hoped for such
strong affirmative feelings toward her, than she would have been by
softly spoken regrets. It seemed incumbent upon her, for Julian's
sake alone, to present the facts that he seemed to be brushing away.

"I cannot quite believe that you know what you're saying, pleasant though it is to my ears," she told him weakly.

"My brother and his wife would be overjoyed to see you," he said.
"I have been in communication with them over the recent week."

"No doubt they aren't aware of what has happened to my for-
tunes in The City almost overnight."

"That, dearest Heather, is entirely a parochial matter."

"The scandal in which I find myself enmeshed is likely to reach
beyond Norfolk," she disagreed. "Nothing pleases people in the
British Isles like an example of immorality, preferably among the
Fashionables. My mother had a friend named Maud McThrapple,
whose downfall with a stranger at Hawick has been constant source
of warning from her to me."

"Nonetheless, Heather, I haven't come here to discuss the woes
of Miss Maud McThrapple, frightful though they must have been."
He was finding it difficult to poise himself on his legs. "You must
visit on the next week's end and meet my only surviving immediate
family. I feel sure they will be as fond of you as I am, though in
different ways, of course."

"The natives and all of London will feel certain that, immoral
wench as I am, my attentions have shifted from the wicked Ambrose Pennymore to you. It will be accepted as common gossip that
we are in the throes of a physical affair without benefit of clergy."

He did not flinch from the truth of her observation. "If so, other
men are going to be envious of me."

"It will be unfortunate for your career in the House of Lords."

"No, it would exalt my career," he said doggedly.

Heather recognized the desire to make another person happy and reveled in it. Nonetheless the truth had to be spoken. Mamma had raised her to be honorable, and she felt an obligation to the man who wanted to marry her.

"People of importance would feel certain that you had descended into the gutter to find a woman. They would say that you were elevating a virtual—dollymop, as I think the word is."

"And in the event of marriage between us?" he asked quietly.

"Then, in their estimation, you would have married your dollymop, but that wouldn't make you a more respected member of Parliament, my dear."

"I am sure that you exaggerate."

She shook her head firmly. Enough experience of London and the various ways of its fashionable citizens had been accumulated by her over the last two years to make an expert of Heather Shaw.

"You are hurting both of us," he said.

She turned away from him, something she never thought she would do. It was not with this intention that she had waited to see him and hoped for his love. Again she had to face the simple truth of scandal and all its repercussions in her life and his, more by far than he was aware of.

"Do you think that the passing of time will make it possible for us to declare our feelings toward each other?" he asked, having used the silence to consider her words and now making it clear that he wasn't in agreement with them.

"I hope so." She spoke quietly. "I pray so."

"Do you mean that when we are both old we will be able to collapse into each other's arms?" He was speaking with a bitterness that Heather didn't suppose she would often hear from him. "I cannot accept a word of this, not one solitary word."

"Julian, have you no idea what it means to me that I must be saying these things?" Her face twisted. "In time, with new scandals replacing this one, what has happened to me will be forgotten. When our feelings are made manifest, then, your widsom in the

Lords will be known to others and the damage cannot be considered of much importance."

He shook his head fiercely. No doubt he imagined all ridicule as unimportant, all opposition brushed away by directness and the love he had never before experienced.

"There is not much time to discuss it today, I fear. I have promised to resume being painted by your brother, which I hadn't expected at this time. He wants the morning sunlight as a conspirator to his deed, I gather. After that, I must go off to the Lords and may be involved in preparing legislation through some of the night. However, you and I will discuss these matters again, Heather, have no misapprehension about that."

She didn't see him leave. Alone, as before, she refrained from tears. It offered not the least consolation that she had followed Mamma's advice to act as a friend, and followed the injunctions she had received from childhood to behave honorably. Being so dutiful a daughter had this time not made her a whit happier.

Mrs. Shaw was pacing back and forth from the front of Heather's room to that of the small sitting room above, hands behind her, head slightly forward. At sight of her serious-visaged daughter, however, she straightened and advanced.

"Is anything wrong?"

"Yes."

Heather, in no mood for the long discussion she imagined would be forthcoming, had started to her room.

"Halt at this very minute and tell me what took place."

A confrontation was unavoidable, and Heather didn't care if it happened in the hall.

"You have given me much advice over the years about the way I should order my life, and I took that advice. I did what was proper and honorable."

Mrs. Shaw said quietly, "You mean that to be a criticism of my teachings."

"In a way, and yet I couldn't have done anything else, for whatever reason, in dealing with Julian."

"Now that you are apparently willing to discuss matters, Heather, it will be preferable to do so in your own room."

Again she gave in. There was no point to antagonizing Mamma, and inferentially Maurice and possibly even the stones of Brook Street. Mrs. Shaw closed the door on them and waited.

"I told Julian that I could not entertain his proposal as long as I am a figure of scandal and he an untried solon," Heather said. "I felt it would be disastrous for him."

"Yes, I see." Mrs. Shaw bit her lower lip briefly, reddening it. "And what was his response?"

"He wishes to pursue the matter as soon as may be," Heather said. "I do not."

"Would he be willing to wait for you? No, don't answer. Of course he would, but there are many attractive women in this infernal settlement and his affections might soon be engaged elsewhere. Particularly if he is a solon who shows signs of being useful to the Empire."

Heather had winced in spite of herself at hearing this truth spoken so calmly.

"Of course he will always love you, but there are considerations other than unrequited passion," said Mrs. Shaw, looking to one side at a representation of two children hand-in-hand. "One hardly knows what to say in the face of a daughter's loyalty to those principles with which she was raised. It is altogether rare and touching in this world."

Heather caught the burgeoning sarcasm in Mrs. Shaw's tones. "Should I have done anything else?"

"No. No, I suppose not," Mamma had to admit, eyes downcast. "Where are you off to?"

Heather had taken a silver-edged cape and was adjusting it in front of the mirror.

"Almost certainly to see Augusta Satterthwaite."

The planned visit might make these daylight hours somewhat endurable. Miss Satterthwaite was a friend who always seemed to be unoccupied during the day. Her nights, according to gossip which Heather was inclined to accept, were decidedly interesting. The advantages of not being reported by one of the gossip papers or being unable to sketch were very real to her. In the public mind, Augusta Satterthwaite was one of those respectable young females who would abhor the wicked deeds of someone like Heather Shaw. Nor would there be any discussion of such matters in the other girl's company.

"I should have guessed your plans." Mrs. Shaw forced herself to change the subject. "Ask Augusta about nitrous oxide, which is supposed to extract teeth painlessly or make it possible for a dental surgeon to do so. She's had the process employed upon her, and I'd like to know the details."

"Yes, Mamma."

Mrs. Shaw paused at the door. "You did do what was right, child," she said softly, her speech reverting to what was, after all, uppermost on her mind. "I don't know that it offers much satisfaction at night in a lonely room, but I can say nothing more."

Heather impulsively wanted to embrace Mamma once more in friendship and family love, but the latter was already in the hall.

From there, the matriarch of the clan proceeded downstairs. She called Beryl to one side and gave the distraught maid one month's notice that she was losing her situation. It was plain that Beryl had been the catalyst for the difficulties that were plaguing all three Shaws in varied fashions.

"You are being well treated," Mrs. Shaw said truthfully in response to Beryl's look as if she had been crushed. "One hundred years ago, had you done any such mischief as you perpetrated, you would almost certainly have had your head cut off."

"Oh no, ma'am." Beryl couldn't help putting both hands up protectively to her throat.

"Yes indeed," Delphine Shaw insisted. "Although I am a firm believer in justice tempered with mercy, there have been times in the last hours when I have wondered just how much progress our civilization has really made."

And on that note, Mrs. Shaw turned away to perform such other duties as could be found that would occupy her time.

CHAPTER FIFTEEN

A Ball Is Planned Under Protest

Miss Florence Nightingale raised her hands at the finish, accepting well-deserved applause. She had been discoursing against the recently concluded Crimean War, the wickedness of officialdom, the bondage in which women were held by their society, and the need for England to be organized afresh on almost every level. The small gaunt Miss Nightingale, zealous to redress injury, dedicated to reform, passionate without love, offered an unsettling image of a middle-aged woman lacking husband or child.

Sir Samuel looked at his daughter sitting at the left in this crowded auditorium. Admiring Florence Nightingale though Clarissa did, she had applauded only perfunctorily.

No doubt she was preoccupied. Her father, who had brought her because it was the sort of speechmaking he felt sure his daughter would relish, knew why Clarissa remained disturbed.

His own dislike of the gossip papers which had made a scandalous figure out of one young man she respected and admired was matched by none. Let a Bank Charter act be put through, or the London-Birmingham Railway be built, or the Royal Exchange burn down and the gift of reading might never have been bestowed as far as gossip sheet news was concerned. Those editors weren't like that pouter-pigeon of a John Thadeus Delane in Printing House Square, respected editor of *The Times* and arbiter of tasteful reporting.

The banishment of Sir John Conroy, the resignation of Melbourne as First Minister in favor of a factory-owner's favorite, Bobby Peel, would earn only a few sticks of type, as the printers called it, to recollect only two major historical developments of Sir

Samuel's time. No uprising in Paris with Louis Napoleon impris-
oned, or war between Turk and Syrian, no, not even a British set-to
with heathen Chinese about opium would truly interest those read-
ers.

On the other hand, let a wicked new Parisian dance appear, the
Cancan, and silver-salt daguerre reproductions of degenerate Frogs
could be printed up by the hundred thousands. Let the Queen
marry some tailor's dummy from Saxe-Coburg by whom she later
has the first child of many, and extensive details are given. Let a
death occur in the prizefight ring, or the Grand National Steeple-
chase be instituted at Aintree, however, and page after page is devoted to models of inaccurate reporting.

As for the transgressions of men and women in society, the care
and detail given to communicating these matters were indeed considerable.

Not that Sir Samuel's ruminations made him feel better about the
difficulty that had indirectly been caused to Clarissa. For a man like
himself, a man with an eye to advancement as a peer, a man burdened by a lucrative trade which could never be mentioned in polite
society, such a man had to accept the verdict of the multitudes and
proscribe anyone who ran afoul of Mrs. Grundy and her peers. Like
others, he felt some sneaking sympathy and admiration for Ambrose
Pennymore, who didn't seem like a devil with the women, but circumstances had put him beyond the pale. His attraction for Clarissa
and hers for him, no matter what the outcome might have been,
simply meant nothing now.

As a devoted parent Sir Samuel took it upon himself to express
disappointment with his progeny's behavior.

"I brought you here because I felt sure you'd like hearing her," he
said, over diminishing applause. It wasn't necessary to add that his
daughter had spent the last day being unsatisfied with her portion in
life.

Clarissa's blond hair lifted slightly as she tossed her head. "I feel a
very deep admiration for Miss Nightingale, and all that she has
accomplished in the cause of women's equality, but—"

Sir Samuel, who had never given any serious thought to women
being equal or subordinate, fought to keep from expressing an opin-

ion which was not to the point at the present juncture. This time he won.

"—but I cannot think long about Miss Nightingale after the last day's developments in my life."

"You can take your mind off those matters at another place more successfully, I feel sure." He was generally opposed to his daughter's attending music halls, where some of the entertainment verged on what he considered too salacious for her ears. Nonetheless, there was no circumstance so rigid that some exception couldn't be attempted, a proverb he had rarely taken with the appropriate seriousness.

"We can trundle off to Astley's on, I think, Curzon Street," he suggested. "I do believe that Stan Featherstone, the Cockney Laureate as he is called, will be making an appearance."

"Thank you, Father, but I would be poor company," Clarissa said. "Stan Featherstone would be there, but Ambrose wouldn't."

A vision of young Pennymore singing cockney songs from a dais drifted through Sir Samuel's mind. For this frivolity, he briefly reproached himself. Other and more urgent considerations beckoned.

"Nonetheless, that is where we are going," he said firmly. "I'll see to it that you are diverted from your dismals, my dear, if it's the last thing I do."

He led his daughter out of the auditorium at last, having waited for the crowd to become thinner. In front of the rabbit-warren he looked around for the family brougham, his glance taking in Bow Street and the stalls on the Long Acre. A gray and white horse bus passed by slowly enough for a funeral train, the animals' heads bowed as if in mourning. Fog, which had come and gone over the last days, was returning. Almost everything in sight looked as if it had suddenly grown a set of Dundreary whiskers.

His curve-patterned brougham materialized at the curbing. Sir Samuel had proudly purchased it from F. and R. Shanks at Lincoln's Inn Fields during the week he was knighted.

"Father, I will not enter a music hall tonight," Clarissa said firmly as she eased herself into the Shankses product without help. One time when it had tilted grotesquely as she was making an entrance, she had referred to the conveyance scornfully as the Shankses mare's nest. Her proud father had retold the story in business circles, but noted, too, that Clarissa had never again lost her balance in the vehicle.

It would have been far from advisable to drag her into Astley's, and unthinkable for a man in his position to cause a scene. Sir Samuel's occupation might make him almost immune to the sort of agitations that were sparking the financial markets in Europe because of the misbehavior of railroads in the United States, but his ambition for a baronetcy could be compromised by public scenes. He knew he wasn't the only lion of industry whose dealings with family members made him feel like a budgerigar.

"Hang it, Clarissa, there must be something reasonable you would like to do!"

"At the moment only to go home and sleep."

Clarissa's tone was too melodramatic as a barometer of feelings. As she could be fertile with suggestions Sir Samuel felt that she was maneuvering him into a position where agitation would cause him to give way on some outrageous demand if his daughter's behavior would only return to normal.

"All right," he said as the carriage began a tortuous return to Bennet Street. "What do you want?"

"Father, I don't understand!" But a telltale gleam in her late mother's forest green eyes gave Clarissa away.

Seasoned negotiator that he was, Sir Samuel felt justified in snorting skeptically.

"There is something you want from me, some horrendous plan in which I am to follow your lead. You expect me to be so concerned for your health that I will give in to any wild scheme of yours." Warningly he raised a thick hand. "However, society will not permit me to tolerate young Ambrose as a son-in-law."

Clarissa winced but resumed communicating that she suffered beyond words.

"I am adamant about that, you may be sure, Clarissa."

"An idea has just come to me."

"I'll bet it came hours ago, and when I hear it I'm going to wish it could be sent away."

"If there was a public occasion at our home, a party of some kind, a ball, for example—"

" 'For example'? Why stop at a ball? Why not a contest between Christians and lions imported from Africa and given to the Regent's Park zoo? That would be sufficiently spectacular in my judgment."

"A ball," Clarissa continued serenely, "where everyone would see Ambrose with me and know from the sweetness of his look that he has done nothing sordid."

"Your certainty that a human's features will be viewed as an index to his or her level of depravity is not one that I share," Sir Samuel said with surprising temperateness. "Even if I went so far as to agree to holding a ball in my home, an invasion of privacy unparalleled in my experience, I can think of one male who would not make an appearance on the premises."

"Consider that the flower of London's fashionable set might appear and welcome Ambrose."

"The flower, indeed! They'll certainly appear, being people who would crawl on hands and knees over broken bottles to get a meal for themselves. But they will not accept someone who isn't going to be present."

Clarissa wisely retreated to a previously prepared position. "You have an excellent chance to offer a night's refuge to people of importance and influence in London town."

Those last words had been shrewdly chosen. Sir Samuel imagined the possibility of taking some Lord or royal equerry to one side and sounding out that dignitary on the subject of his chances for soon becoming a Baronet. Many of these people would be in his debt after a night's *ridotto*. As a businessman, but not a socially adept personage, it struck Sir Samuel that he ought to have discussed such a course with his daughter in the past.

"I shall supervise the invitation list, however," he insisted, managing the not unknown parental feat of belligerently acceding to a descendant's demands. "There will be no sign of young Pennymore among the revelers at my board. I still am in possession of a horse-whip and a strong right arm, Clarissa, and am fully prepared to apply both in case of need."

Clarissa, however, was only slightly cast down. It must be possible somehow to arrange for guests to approach Sir Samuel about the good points of Ambrose Pennymore, his honesty, his uprightness. Such words from those who might help him obtain a baronetcy would be of considerable use in gaining Ambrose's hand in marriage, as she thought of it. Accordingly, Clarissa began making plans for the notable occasion and didn't feel at all dissatisfied about what she had accomplished on this night.

CHAPTER SIXTEEN

Two Strategic Retreats and One Strategic Advance

A note addressed to Heather was acquired by Maurice on Thursday at midmorning and brought to her in the large sitting room. She was in Mamma's company and watching the interview of the first maid sent out by the Piercey Domestic Service Agency on Bow Street. Beryl, the maid who had been under a cloud and thoroughly humiliated by recent events, hadn't paused to collect that part of a pay packet which would have been due her, but had simply run off.

Heather observed that the writing on the envelope wasn't masculine and therefore not Julian's. Putting the missive to one side on the nearest table and beneath a triptych of underexposed photographs, she continued listening to the interview.

This prospective maid, a small and ferret-faced creature, was apparently determined on gaining sympathy. To that end, she had embarked on recounting the story of her life. "Me mum took me to a cousin 'oo was a butler and 'e put me to work. Mum, expecting she would die very quick with the consumption, kissed me once on the cheek, the right cheek, a wet kiss, an' then she went off from the belowstairs kitchen. I remember she coughed all the while she was 'alf-walkin' and 'alf-runnin' to the door. Even on the other side she coughed. I can remember 'er frizzy gray 'air, not so bright as yours, ma'am. 'aunted she looked, with shadows under the eyes an' that cough what never stopped. As for me dad, I 'ardly knew 'im, what with—"

"Just so," Mamma said, calling into play a degree of tact of which

Heather hadn't felt sure she was capable. Mother and daughter exchanged glances. Mrs. Shaw shook her head.

"A milksop," Mamma said, having first told the young woman that Mrs. Piercey would be notified of the family decision and seen her leave. "If anything ever went wrong in the house after that one was hired, we would be hearing tearful excuses till the last trump."

"She *has* had a difficult life."

"So have many others, but they only discuss it among family and friends," Mrs. Shaw said briskly. "Heather, you fully concur with the decision and the reasons for it, but you are trying to make me feel like an ogre for doing what is necessary for our happiness."

It was true enough. Heather apologized with a smile and wondered how many times in the past she had adopted stances which were unreasonable in given circumstances.

The second candidate was not a whiner, but she did happen to be an Amazon. Indeed, she was one of the biggest humans Heather had ever encountered.

"Under no circumstances would you fit the uniforms, I fear," Mamma said regretfully. Running up new clothes for this one would be an expense, but not an awesome one. Mamma chose a time to consult Heather when it could only be done wordlessly.

Maurice, having been in and out of the room, looked at the Amazon while she was departing. "I couldn't easily tolerate a maid who looks as if she'd be able to pick me up when in a fit of pique and hurl me out a window."

Mamma nodded, and Heather now realized that the particular objection had been anticipated. For the second time in half an hour, Heather felt abashed.

The third contender was a small but supple-looking young woman. With a tuck here and there, she would fit Beryl's uniforms. More importantly, Mrs. Shaw, like Heather, was wearying of the confrontations with lower orders.

"And your name? No, I could not call you Queenie. A maid named Queenie would be intolerable." Mamma considered. "If you are accepted for the position, you will be named—ah—Bridget."

"Beg pardon, mum, but I'm not Irish."

"A minor objection. I have always liked the name of Bridget for a maid."

Maurice, who had briefly wandered in as the sun faded through his attic, thereby prohibiting him from painting a street scene for his own pleasure, chuckled. If Heather guessed correctly, he would have enjoyed a household with a maid called Queenie. Nothing would have better suited his strange sense of fun.

"You will be on trial for two weeks, earning two-and-six the day," said Mrs. Shaw. She had looked at her spawn for concurrence only if she didn't want to hire someone, but with her mind settled she acted without the formality of seeking guidance. "Today, primarily, you will be shown the house by Mrs. Fisher, the cook, and your duties will be explained to you afterward. Mrs. Fisher understands matters."

"Yes, mum."

Heather would have expected Mamma to be discomfited by the recollection of the first maid, who had referred to her consumptive parent with the same intonation. Mrs. Shaw apparently didn't notice the similarity.

"Tonight you are to serve the dinner and attend the cleaning afterward. I will now lead you in to see Mrs. Fisher, who will take charge of your education."

Heather was opening the day's missive at last as Mrs. Shaw left with the maid respectfully in tow. The signature could be deciphered as Clarissa's. Expecting to read a litany of sadness from that demoiselle, who had never before experienced a romance let alone been thwarted in one, Heather hesitated to plunge into the letter. Just as she was deciding to undertake that feat, the door opened on Mamma's return.

"I am not hopeful, but something has to be done about service for tonight," she said, looking from one child to another. Having made it clear that she had acted against her will and could be excused no matter what might go wrong, Mamma sat down.

"Something else has to be done," Maurice said firmly, looking into his mother's eyes although she was seated and he stood with legs defiantly apart close to the tile mantel register, the top of his head on a line with the top of the overmantel mirror.

"I don't know what you mean," Mamma said justifiably.

"If the Frenchies can have arc-lighting in their new opera house," Maurice responded, somewhat mysteriously at first, "we can have a butler. It looks better for a painter's home and gives an air of respectability. I was reluctant to say anything because commissions had been coming so easily, but now I think it will be useful to make that change."

"And what of the expense?"

"I have earned considerable money before and will do so again," Maurice said a little belligerently.

Such a course was adopted, although none of the Shaws looked forward to further *pourparlers* with possible employees. Nonetheless the afternoon was spent in discussion with butlers thin and portly, butlers with much experience and little, butlers with arthritis or drinking problems, butlers too young or long past their most active years.

At one point, Heather was able to return her attention to Clarissa's letter. The first paragraph began with the words, *You will have heard, of course, about my difficulties over Ambrose, for which, you may be sure, I do not hold you in the least responsible.* Heather sniffed at such breathtaking disregard of another's woes and put the missive to one side. There would be time to peruse that garland afterward, of course.

The supper, with soup, remove, poultry and two vegetables, entrées, and dessert with tea, was served by Bridget-née-Queenie under the sharp eye of Mr. Sparrow, the butler, who had thoughtfully provided one uniform for himself and obtained the situation because such covering was available. He seemed competent, as did the fine-drawn Bridget.

The guests, of course, were unaware of any possible difficulties. A new client of Maurice's, Sir Thomas Jolley, was a large-voiced and energetic man with the habit of command. His wife was smaller and thinner, but her sharp voice testified to a capacity for indignation which had no doubt been visited over the years upon Sir Thomas and their seven children. Neither guest made reference to the simmering scandal that involved Heather, as Sir Thomas was interested only in commissioning a portrait of himself to be used on labels for the commercial product he manufactured.

At one point he told Heather in some detail how he had conceived his Universal pill on the London-to-Bath train run while the machine was halting to replenish its water tanks and passengers stretched their legs. Sir Thomas would have died before admitting that the nostrum contained nothing but animal fats and compressed vegetables.

Social conversation after the meal took a little longer. Maurice finally escorted Sir Thomas and Lady Jolley to their carriage. Heather, drifting into the large sitting room, worked her way past houseplants and ostrich feathers in decorated vases, a whatnot infested with bric-a-brac, fans on the walls, pillows and chairs placed demonically to irritate residents and impede progress, needless candle holders, and mirrors. Clarissa's letter had been shifted from a small table to the mantel register. Reminded by the sight that her friend's *cri de coeur* had not yet been read in its entirety, Heather settled herself to the labor.

As soon as she discovered from further reading that the letter had been smuggled out via a trusty maid, Heather felt encouraged. Clarissa wasn't merely pining away. Heather had done this friend an injustice and now attempted to remedy it by reading more swiftly.

There was a smile on her face when she put the letter to one side. Like Clarissa herself on the previous night, she started making plans.

When Maurice wandered into the large sitting room, rubbing his hands because terms for the commission had finally been agreed upon, Heather was in wait.

"Would you like to spend a few hours outdoors?" She smiled at the nearly profane exclamation that crossed her brother's lips. "Let me tell you in the fewest possible words why you should change your mind."

Sister and brother arrived at the frozen lake in St. James's Park before midnight. Various servants were carrying lighted torches, which permitted anyone to look west at Buckingham Palace or south in the direction of Birdcage Walk. Heather felt too preoccupied to avail herself of such pleasures.

On the frozen lake itself, skaters disported themselves. Others sat around bonfires. Vendors of knicknacks could be heard crying the wares they offered. Others had set up booths for the purpose of selling hot meats, hot pies, roasted chestnuts, or buttered rum.

Heather, adjusting herself to the cumbersome wooden footplates from which long rounded heels made it possible to navigate the ice, moved slowly at first. Maurice, by her side, prepared to stare down any who might look censoriously at his scandal-tinged sister, was humming along with a mildly bawdy ditty being chanted by several young men nearby, one of whom was tormenting a stringed instrument.

"There, at the left, is Augusta Satterthwaite," Maurice, ever sharp-eyed, remarked.

"I will discuss matters with her," Heather said, glancing significantly toward her brother by way of a prelude.

Moving slowly by herself, she approached Miss Satterthwaite. The befurred and bespangled beauty, not bothering to skate, was surrounded by five young men and resented being called to one side. It would have seemed churlish to those admirers, however, if she had refused.

"Please be quick," she said imperiously in a voice unlike the one she favored for discourse with males. "I don't want to lose Cyril Jenkinson, and please remember that he came to me first."

Heather had no interest in the Jenkinson issue, the young man in question being one of the more arrogant London peacocks.

"Augusta, there is going to be a ball given next weekend by Sir Samuel Fitton in his daughter's honor. Can I assume that your parents will escort you to the function?"

"Almost certainly they will insist on doing so." Miss Satterthwaite crinkled her pretty nose, disapproving of parents who upheld standards. "Why do you ask about this?"

"I want you to persuade your father to take Sir Samuel aside, if only briefly, and find some excuse to mention how much he likes and admires Ambrose Pennymore."

The elder Satterthwaite's shoe-blacking enterprise had been put on its feet by the Pennymore Bank. It would be astonishing if the man didn't have the highest regard for the founders of the feast.

"I doubt if my father ever dealt with Ambrose, but I'll ask for the favor." Augusta looked surprised. "Why are you anxious for someone to speak so highly to another about your gentleman friend?"

Only with difficulty did Augusta repress a series of giggles. Certainly she, too, had been exposed to the infamous issue of *Society Deeds*, and probably told some other intimates how much more careful she was in her adventures than the Scots girl. She had hinted as much at their previous meeting.

The query had been phrased so slightingly that Heather didn't answer.

As much as Augusta wanted to return to the pride of males awaiting her, she paused to ask, "And what *do* you see in Ambrose Pennymore? He always seemed unaware of the ways of women."

Needing the other's assistance with her male parent, Heather had to offer some remark. "Ambrose is one of those still waters who runs very, very deep."

Augusta's mouth was formed in an awed circle as she turned back to her party.

It was impossible to know if the elder Satterthwaite would further the plans Clarissa had made and for which Heather was being the only possible amanuensis. Maurice looked in her direction, brows raised to discover if she had been successful in dealing with Augusta. Despite the furred cape with which Heather was burdened for the chill February night, she pantomimed a shrug.

Moving slowly in his direction to ask if he might find another who could be approached, she was herself accosted by the handsome Claude Yellowlees. She wanted to turn away, recollecting Claude as having been one of those young men who had snickered at her while she sat with Clarissa watching the Prince Consort decorate several brave men at Hyde Park two days ago. Memory informed her, however, that Claude was a nephew of Herbert Yellowlees, the Duke of Blackwall.

Before Claude could speak, perhaps with cheap sarcasm, Heather was busily clearing her throat.

"I am certain that your uncle, the Duke, will be invited to Sir Samuel Fitton's ball for his daughter Clarissa. You, too, are likely to be asked."

"Perhaps." Thick smoke left Claude's mouth as he drawled.

"I need a favor that I don't want anyone else to know about except your uncle," she said. "Request the Duke to speak quietly with Sir Samuel at the ball and say good things about Ambrose Pennymore. After all, the Pennymore Bank has loaned money to him, from the gossip everyone has heard, and praise from a peer will be praise indeed."

Claude was startled, not aware of any reason for Heather's wanting that particular favor. She looked serious. Instead of making a remark that might have caused her to embarrass him publicly, therefore, Claude gave the matter some thought.

"My uncle won't attend unless his health allows, and that is not often the case nowadays."

"His health?"

"I could recite to you a list of his ailments no shorter than the road from St. James's Park to Samarkand."

"Can it be arranged for him to seek out Sir Samuel's company in The City and do the necessary thing?"

"He rarely leaves his own hearth."

"Will you ask, then, for him to write a letter along the lines I indicate?"

"My uncle's hand isn't what it was when he considered himself a stripling of forty, and as a result he rarely essays a communication of that sort."

"Someone in the family could write a letter and he could sign it." Heather was beginning to approach desperation in the search for remedies.

"His eyesight isn't of the best and he could hardly decipher what had been written. Certainly he would be reluctant to add his fist as a result."

If Heather had not been standing on skates over ice she would have thrown up her hands. "Claude, you are totally useless!"

"Largely, perhaps, but not totally."

Leaving the company of Claude Yellowlees in the gingerly way forced upon her because of the mode by which she moved, Heather encountered Sylvan Dorward. Mr. Dorward was a young man whose features reminded her of Sir Samuel Fitton's bulldog, the ineffable

Dizzy. At the moment, Mr. Dorward's snuffling accented the resemblance. Although she was far from besotted by the young man, particularly now that he was finishing the last of a meat pie obtained from one of the nearby booths, Heather stopped him and even ventured on a smile. Mr. Dorward, no doubt considering the smile to mean more than it did, halted rather than continue wavering, and swallowed a huge morsel of pie at once.

"I wonder if you would agree to do me a favor," Heather began as winningly as she could manage, although she looked at a point over Mr. Dorward's head as she spoke. "You are a friend of Lord Junor's, are you not?"

"Indeed I am," Mr. Dorward said proudly.

Heather made her request once more, using the fewest possible words and capping them with a smile.

"It is most irregular," Sylvan Dorward said automatically. "I have never heard of Junor being asked anything quite like this, and it will be difficult to put it to him. Extremely difficult, I may add. If, of course, I choose to do so."

Heather was on the point of saying that she would rather not, on second thoughts, put Mr. Dorward to such a mountainous challenge.

"However—" He smiled in turn, now that the pie was safely down among his innards. "For you, Heather, I will do the best that is in me."

Such a willingness to oblige was astonishing from this source. Heather soon understood, however, why Mr. Dorward, like the fabled leopard, had apparently changed his spots. The man smiled winningly at this girl who was officially considered to be disreputable.

"As I am going to do something for you and your good friend," he said in what was more of a smirking voice than a speaking one, "I hope that you will accordingly do something for me."

Heather's pulling back made it clear that she would find other means to assist Ambrose and Clarissa. Mr. Dorward's lips suddenly lost their tentative smile.

It was best to leave with alacrity, and this was what Heather attempted to do. The speed with which she moved caused her to founder, however, and imperilled her balance.

Maurice, watching, started forward to be of aid, and then suddenly halted.

Two strong hands, circling Heather's midriff from the back, kept her upright. Not knowing who had rescued her, Heather nonetheless straightened herself. Only then, moving with a slowness that would have been to advantage a moment before, she saw the man who had been so helpful.

Julian was smiling affectionately at her.

"Are you able to stand on your own?"

"Indeed I am, thank you."

"Oh." He looked regretful. "I had hoped that you would remain a helpless pawn of the elements, needing guidance and a firm hand at every step."

"At the moment that isn't so," she said, feeling regretful about it herself. The memory of his sturdy but gentle arms around her midriff was making her tingle. "Eventually, though, I shall age and be uncertain in my movements, at which time I will require considerable aid on the ice."

"By then, I may not be able to reach the ice," Julian confessed, but there was a glint in his deep brown eyes and he apparently chose not to confront the prospect of eventual helplessness.

"Meanwhile you frolic," she said with mock severity.

He became more serious. "I am here with the Marquis of Evindale, with whom I have spent all evening in a discussion of the second reading of a bill to be held at the Waxworks tomorrow afternoon."

"Discussions of such gravity are not meant to take place where gravity itself poses some difficulties," Heather grinned.

Again he looked as if he had been accused of a nameless crime. "I have planned to visit your brother's *atelier* tomorrow morning and to see you as well, but I am happy to see you in advance, too." He wavered on his own skates and looked down a little irritably at them. "These I purchased at one of the booths. I must tell you that the skates crafted in Norfolk are far more sturdy."

His moment's seriousness caused Heather to recall urgent matters. "I have been occupied with a difficulty as a result of our own worries. You must realize that I feel some guilt for the dilemma that Ambrose Pennymore faces in being under a cloud in the eyes of fashionable society."

"Of course." Although he hadn't known her a long time, Julian was well aware that she would feel strongly about obligations which had to be settled. "Do you propose to reclaim Ambrose Pennymore?"

"Indeed yes."

"You would hardly seem in a position to accomplish that goal, worthy though it may be."

She glanced around as if she contemplated some mild profanity at the expense of the Fashionables, and didn't want it overheard.

At Julian's instigation she began skating once more, her confidence bolstered by the knowledge that he was close enough to perform another rescue if the need arose. She wanted very much to hold his hands while the two of them were in motion, but because of the current acuteness of London gossip it seemed an unwise procedure at this time.

"Sir Samuel Fitton, Clarissa's father, will be amenable to assisting him if peers and others in the highest reaches of good society first inform Sir Samuel of how highly they respect Ambrose. I may add that many, in fact, do respect him."

"And what form would this knight's helpfulness take?"

"He would become convinced that his public-spirited act in 'forgiving' Ambrose will gain the respect of society despite the gossip. The way will be cleared for him to accept Ambrose into his family by permitting the marriage of Ambrose to Clarissa Fitton, Sir Samuel's only child. I may add that both Ambrose and Clarissa are deeply desirous of such an outcome."

Julian pursed his lips, a gesture that would have been awkward in any other male. It seemed that he was alertly considering the various factors in the equation that had just been put before him.

"I have followed your exposition with great keenness, I believe, my senses having been honed by the protracted study of legislation before it can be dismembered in the House of Lords. Some part of the matter evades my comprehension still."

"Ask your question and I will be happy to elucidate."

"Well, then, why is a successful businessman who has been knighted so very determined to gain the approval of London's influential men?"

He had spoken as an outlander whose own opinion of society members hadn't yet been formed.

"Because," said Heather, "it will aid Sir Samuel in acquiring the baronetcy he covets."

"Ah." Julian's experience with legislation came to his aid. "A *quid pro quo* is desired."

"Your formulation does not understate the position as I understand it," Heather conceded.

"Very well, then, I vote that I am content with the pending action," he said, descending to the use of a term that was probably favored in the Waxworks, as he privately referred to the deliberative body in which he sat. "I am willing to concede the possibility of success in that goal."

"Your aid will be needed along with your good wishes," Heather remarked.

"Ah." Julian's smile put his normally ruddy cheeks into sharp relief by the light of torches. "You are suggesting that I speak to Fitton in praise of the luckless Ambrose."

"Indeed, yes. If you encounter Sir Samuel in the course of your duties in The City, that will give you a perfect opportunity."

"No doubt I can take him to one side and say something like, 'And speaking of the possibility of a war with the Turks, are you aware that Mr. Ambrose Pennymore would make a splendid son-in-law?' "

"A little more subtlety would be appreciated," Heather said drily. Before he could enunciate an equally parodistic approach, she added, "Next weekend Sir Samuel will be giving a ball in honor of his daughter, and the goal can certainly be accomplished there. It is an even worthier objective at this time than visiting your family in Norfolk, as you had suggested."

"I will be happy to be dragooned into giving aid if indeed I am invited to this donnybrook to which you refer."

"You will be. Sir Samuel is assiduously courting, so to speak, all peers whether they are single or married. He has not yet made contact with those who are dead, but it wouldn't surprise me if he initiates an attempt along that order on such short notice as well."

Silence fell between them, companionable on her side and restless on his. Heather was suddenly aware of sniffing singed meat from one of the booths. It was hardly the equal of soft music at a meeting between two who loved each other.

"I am now *au courant,* as we say in Norfolk," Julian resumed, his tone belying the insubstantiality of the words. "However, that is not my only concern, as I am sure you realize."

Heather nodded.

"My most important consideration is one that you must have already anticipated."

That was true. He wanted to know the way matters stood between them.

"After the Pennymore *brouhaha* is resolved and the scandal consigned to the oblivion it so richly deserves," Julian said, choosing his words like a debater reaching a conclusion that must perforce be above dispute, "you will then feel that you can marry me."

He wasn't the man to be deflected from reaching a goal. It was a trait that Heather would have admired at almost any other time.

She wanted to tell him that a favorable outcome for Clarissa and Ambrose, much as she felt duty-bound to assist in providing it, would change nothing in Julian's situation and hers. After all, Ambrose could have been a coxcomb, but his reformation and marriage would make him entirely respectable. A female who was perceived to have been dissolute in her ways, whether or not that was true, could expect no forgiveness as a direct consequence of exchanging vows in marriage.

Let her marry someone not yet respected by society and the conjoining would be taken as proof that the man was unreliable in judgment. Julian, marrying her as quickly as both desired, might never have the opportunity to become a pivotal member of the Lords, the feat he was clearly so anxious to accomplish.

In time, however, when he was perceived as a respected and stable factor in Her Majesty's Government, the marriage would change nothing adversely for him. It was a point she had made to him recently.

"I am not aware of what more is to be said," she now told him with regret he must have perceived. "It will need time, Julian. For your sake, it will need time to keep our marriage from being a cause of dissension between you and your colleagues at the Lords. And perhaps between us as well."

He became still, forcing Heather to stop as he turned stiffly to face her.

"If that is your decision," he said, not accepting a setback one whit more gracefully than in the past. It didn't seem awkward when he bowed slightly from the waist. "I remain your most humble and obedient servant."

Heather watched his broad back as he skated in the opposite direction. Every fiber in her body urged her to call him back despite this public setting in which they found themselves. To refrain from doing so at this time required a mighty effort of will.

CHAPTER SEVENTEEN
Mr. Pennymore Offers Advice

In the house of his father were many rooms, but the business establishment of Leslie Pennymore made do with only a trio of them that were intended for private interviews. The founder of the feast occupied one of these. At the moment he had called his son in for a discussion that didn't involve the business of the bank.

A brief description of Mr. Pennymore, emphasizing only the salient facts, may at this point be useful. The banker was a gentleman whose skin was sallow after many years of working indoors and perusing business statements. His cheeks were bereft of the prominence that Ambrose unwillingly sported. He dressed with an eye toward economy, as he did everything else. The jacket he wore was shy one strategically placed button which had a pattern that wouldn't be rationally duplicated, but there happened to be considerable wear left in the garment.

"Within limits, a young man is expected to be rebellious," Mr. Pennymore began in speaking to his discomfited son. "It is how he recognizes himself as a person apart from his parents."

"Yes, sir."

"However, your recent behavior has been exceedingly disagreeable."

"I beg your pardon, sir?" Ambrose, certain that he had been wronged as few others in the history of Empire, could hardly believe his ears.

"The cause, to be sure, is perfectly natural," Mr. Pennymore said with compassion that gratified his son until an explanation was offered. "At your age a young man requires certain pleasures, certain gratifications. Tell me, Ambrose, have you spent much time with women?"

It would have been difficult to find a more inappropriate query or a less suitable place and moment in which to put it. Nor was his father aware that Ambrose was now considered by many Londoners to be the equal of the late Mr. Casanova. Such ignorance came from leading a sheltered life and involving himself in little beside the business of his bank.

Ambrose couldn't bring himself to answer the question immediately. "I—I have become deeply interested in Miss Clarissa Fitton."

"The daughter of the earth closet entrepreneur?" It was the last way in the world Ambrose would have liked to hear his love referred to. "Didn't know he had one. A respectable girl, I would assume."

"Yes, sir."

Mr. Pennymore gave no sign by word or deed whether he approved of respectable females.

"No doubt time will pass before an arrangement can be made and a marriage, if it materializes, consummated." The elder banker rubbed his hands, probably at the thought of negotiating a large dowry on his son's behalf. "Meanwhile, you urgently require the services of another sort of female."

Ambrose felt himself beyond astonishment. He must have been standing awkwardly, feet apart, hands behind his back. Mr. Pennymore, seated at the pigeonhole desk he favored when foreclosing mortgages or performing other banker duties, was looking thoughtful.

"I feel that I can be of some assistance in the dilemma," Mr. Pennymore said. "With advice, at the start. There are a few things you should remember in seeking female companionship. First, until you are a husband, you will need at some time to employ a strumpet. Doing so can aid your own outlook on life when a decent woman is unavailable."

"Yes, Father." Ambrose's voice sounded as if he was strangling. Few sentiments could have been more inappropriate to him now.

"A few other points. An expenditure of more than two shillings for that purpose would be foolhardy. As for an extra payment afterward, that is entirely at your discretion. Whatever your choice, it is not necessary to make a large additional payment."

Ambrose wasn't surprised that his father's advice about women would boil down to urging economy upon him.

"At some time you may encounter a woman who is not of the strumpet class, but might wish to enjoy congress with you. I can see no objection to a single man beguiling himself in his need. However, it must be made plain that you have no intention of purchasing an establishment for such a creature in St. John's Wood or elsewhere." Mr. Pennymore threw up his hands in horror at the thought. "You will have been beggared in no time, my boy. I see no need to further belabor that point. Or, frankly, anything else I have said. My advice speaks for itself and is well meant, you may be sure."

"Yes, Father, thank you."

Ambrose was shaking himself like a wet dog when he was eventually permitted to leave his father's demesne. It seemed that no discussion could help reminding him of his agonizing difficulties in eventually marrying Clarissa. He could not have known that plans were already afoot to alleviate his suffering, and indeed might not have put his faith in them if he had been informed accordingly. As a man in love, he saw every part of his life in relation to one female. The recent episode, which would have made him shrug or chuckle at any other time, had instead been a grotesque irritant.

To escape, if only for an afternoon, he embarked early on one of the innumerable business trips he had to make in approving loan possibilities for the bank. At least he would be far away from the difficulties of the last days, far, far away.

Druid Street in Bermondsey was lined by old buildings with filthy windows and dirt-choked gutters. The wind carried a smell of fish from the West India Docks. The only person on the street at this time was a red-chinned bake-and-boil man. "Warm yer belly fer 'alf a penny," this worthy called out. The street cry was vulgar enough to make any banker wince, but on Druid Street it was more than welcome.

Ambrose would have felt his father's disapproval if the latter had known about his having hired a cab when a horse bus was available.

He occasionally acted in secret against Leslie Pennymore's implicit directives.

"In which direction is number two-three-one?" he asked the street tradesman.

"On the next block, guv'nor," said the latter. He added, with the fondness of some uneducated persons for long words when not needed, "Just foller your pro-bos-cis, an' yer can't miss the 'ouse."

Ambrose moved even more quickly than he might have done otherwise, glancing from left to right as he walked.

In one window he caught a glimpse of what looked like some huge animal. A surprised second look showed that it was made of metal and bounded by wood. Back of a wooden barrier on the far side stood the man who had spoken to him at the bank, requesting a loan. A long look at the dirt-pocked number plate confirmed the correctness of Ambrose's impression.

He plunged into the dim hall, his nose crinkling at the odors that assailed it. He was reminded of the summer of the great stink, back in '55, with Parliament screening its windows and hardly a curtain not drenched in chloride of lime. Laborers had sealed sewer openings along the Thames between Putney and Blackwell, relieving the ghastly conditions at some cost to the city treasury, as Mr. Leslie Pennymore had pointed out with disapproval.

"'Ere you are, sir," Walter Nisbet said undeniably, in a cheerful voice. "Come in an' 'ave yerself a dekko at the beauty."

Ambrose had made the trip for that very purpose. Nisbet had approached the bank to request a loan for engaging in commerce with the object, which he had inherited from a brother.

A day without sight of any machine that disseminated print would have suited Ambrose very well, he belatedly realized. Because of his own shortsightedness, it was not to be. To his mind, however, this press was of a primitive type not generally in use any longer.

"Yer can see 'ow good it is," Nisbet said with confidence. He was a spare man in ill-fitting clothes. "It says right 'ere."

Leaning over, Ambrose made out the words *Stanhope Invenit*. He looked up at Nisbet, and didn't know he had slightly smiled till he saw a flush on the other's features.

"To tell the truth, Mr. Pennymore, I personally never learned 'ow to read 'cause I didn't need to. So 'ere I am with me future 'angin' on a printin' press. Short of askin' a blind man to pick out colors for the Prince Consort's wardrobe, I can 'ardly think on anythin' less likely. But I'll make it work, you see if I don't. I got chums, that I 'ave!'"

Hardly had that claim been made than somebody was knocking on the door. Nisbet admitted an ugly and overweight man who promptly examined the object that dominated this room.

"It's a Stan'ope," the expert confirmed, needlessly from Ambrose's view, eyes darting back and forth as he pulled at his luxurious moustache. "Been all 'a ten years since I see one 'a these, but I used to run such. The two-sized platen—this 'ere!—gives extra power which means yer can print a form at one ruddy pull."

"I think summat be missin'," Nisbet confessed a little awkwardly. Attempts to check the machine's working capacity had caused type jumbles in the form box.

"Arrgh!" the expert said, probably in agreement. "Somebody took the rounce 'andle, that's sure." A dirty finger pointed above the platen. "It'd be right there, y' see."

"Where can we get another?"

"At the store, 'a course. You goes in an' you says, 'La-dee-da, I wants the best rounce 'andle for a twenty-year-old ruddy Stan'ope as nobody uses no more, and 'ang the expense!' "

"Stow that," Nisbet growled. "I'm willin' to pay a florin for one good rounce on delivery."

" 'Alf a crown and maybe we could make a go."

" 'Alf a crown if I gets it in twenty-four hours."

"Don't want much, does yer?" the expert grumbled on the way out, but he was hurrying.

Ambrose, who had listened approvingly to the businesslike Nisbet, waited until the door had slammed shut. He refused to look at the machine again for reasons that seemed to him entirely cogent, but asked the one question he ought to have posed originally. No doubt he had been too upset to do so back at the bank.

"How do you plan upon using the press?" he began gingerly. "I mean, what will you print on it?"

"News," said Walter Nisbet promptly. "Details about Queen

Vicky 'aving been given chloroform during the birth of 'er next young 'un, for instance." He glanced sharply at Ambrose, not caring whether it was considered that the canons of good taste were being defied. "An' the facts of that triple murder in Clapham—you know, where the man with the ax put the victim into three buckets, though why it took three I never will know."

Ambrose felt queasy, but not only at this reminder of logistical puzzles in the wilds of Clapham.

"After the paper is a success—an' it will be, mind!—I won't take on Mr. Julius Reuter's news service. The reader I'll sell to, 'e don't want to know about prices 'a stocks, but about prices that some fences are payin' for stolen goods. 'Ow I wish I could print summat of that nature in my paper."

"And what about news of society difficulties?" Ambrose was feeling more and more uncomfortable.

"Oh, absolutely. Everybody is interested in that sort 'a racketing."

With so much understood, Ambrose left after making only the most perfunctory excuses. Walter Nisbet was an ambitious man who would accomplish great things in his chosen nefarious vocation. Ambrose would have to recommend that a loan be put through to improve the man's situation. But he, Ambrose, would not deal directly with Walter Nisbet. There were limits beyond which a civilized man didn't venture. Certainly not a man who had himself been victimized by an organ of the type that Nisbet was planning to market.

It was early afternoon, but after such a meeting he would go home and write another letter to Clarissa. No doubt it wasn't going to be delivered past Argus-eyed Sir Samuel, but Ambrose could think of nothing else to do. He was totally disinclined, for once in his life, to take on any further bank business.

At home, to his surprise and delight, he found a letter from the most important source in all the world. It had been awaiting him for hours.

CHAPTER EIGHTEEN

Fresh News at Rotten Row

Undaunted by the cold weather, Ambrose spent much of the late afternoon waiting by Rotten Row in Hyde Park. Here, at the left of horsemen and their female equivalents packed closely together, with servants sometimes trotting along behind if there was room, and the air permeated despite its chill by an odor of ammonia that would have knocked weaker equestrians to the ground, Ambrose paced back and forth.

A Tillbury cab halted some twenty feet from him just as the sun was beginning its descent. Clarissa virtually burst out of the hired cab and ran to where he stood, a uniformed maid pausing out of earshot. Ambrose and Clarissa gazed their respective fills at each other, unmoving for many moments.

Clarissa was in an understandably excitable condition, and not only because she was gazing at the one man above all others to whom she was attracted, the one with whom she had determined to plight her troth despite her father's objections. For the first time she had directly lied to her father, claiming that she would leave the house to fit a gown for the forthcoming ball on the night of Saturday, the twenty-eighth. In pursuit of this goal she had enlisted a maid upon whose loyalty she knew she could rely. As she wasn't given to being untruthful, Clarissa found the resulting tension difficult to bear.

Ambrose, the recipient of a letter smuggled out of the Château d'If at Bennet Street hard by Piccadilly, was rendered wide-eyed by Miss Fitton's blond beauty. Like Clarissa he seemed too unnerved for speaking. This rendezvous was apparently going to be the most secret meeting ever known in the annals of conspiracy, with neither participant momentarily fit for treason, stratagems, or spoils.

Clarissa suddenly felt herself out of breath, however, and inhaled noisily. The sound caused her to realize that some words could appropriately be exchanged at this juncture.

"I am pleased that you received my letter," she said in a voice so low he had to strain before deciphering the words. "And that you took the time from your busy day to see me."

Ambrose still couldn't bring himself to speak, his thoughts being taken by the sight of this vision in the royal blue cape over a pale yellow day dress. Before long, however, he did manage to find a few words.

"Yes. Yes, I am seeing you."

"Quite so." It seemed to Clarissa that they were making progress of a sort, although Ambrose was apparently more satisfied. "I wrote that I had hoped to invite you to a ball my father is giving on the last night of the month."

"I would be honored to attend."

Clarissa didn't click her tongue in dismay at this, realizing that Ambrose had almost certainly not retained a memory of the contents of the letter. She was as happy to see him as he was to see her, but after the first moments her intelligence was working once more.

"My father has vowed to take most unpleasant measures if you appear," she said, confronting the image of a horsewhip uncoiled in the air over Ambrose's fleeing body. "Nonetheless, I expect those who attend, many of them, to speak highly of you."

"Oh." Ambrose had certainly comprehended the last statement, but felt himself distinctly taken aback at hearing it. The prospect of others discussing him was one that he had already faced during the last days, however, and after shying away as if at the sound of a pistol shot, he dredged up a smile and affixed it firmly to his features.

"My friend Heather Shaw—of course you know her!—will make certain that many who respect you and are in attendance at the ball speak to my father in your praise." She looked down modestly. "It was an idea of mine that I believe will be useful."

Ambrose's wide admiring eyes offered proof that he was deeply moved by such social sagacity in the woman he loved. He could only match her clear mental processes by the employment of daring.

"I cannot permit a ball to take place in your honor without my being there, too."

Clarissa looked up. "Oh, you mustn't take any risk for me!"

"I would not take a corresponding risk for anyone else," Ambrose said truthfully. "I will butt my head against the door if necessary to enter, but I shall hold you in my arms and dance with you on that night."

Clarissa, ever practical, spoke with softness. "It is not necessary to dance with a woman in order to hold her."

Ambrose smiled happily and stepped forward to embrace and then kiss her on the lips. Clarissa's arms enclosed him, and she showed no sign of wanting to let go when he had to pause for a breath. Joyously he resumed his activities.

They heard the maid, who was some twenty feet away, suddenly clear her throat. Three times she had to repeat the noise before Ambrose finally broke away.

Clarissa nodded. Satisfied that her feelings for him were reciprocated, a conviction she had ventured out to confirm, she turned to follow the maid back to the waiting Tillbury.

Ambrose looked after the girl he loved, smiling as she turned to wave at him from within the vehicle. Not till she was out of sight did he recollect that he had promised to brave the wrath of Sir Samuel Fitton, possibly antagonizing him forever in order to attend a ball. He might have made an error in prospective tactics, but knew he couldn't possibly do anything else, now.

Maurice Shaw spent the afternoon strolling in Piccadilly with two taller friends. Each man wore high hats and frock coats, white shirts with string ties, and tight pants. Maurice expected nothing more than to see his friends meet young ladies about whom they would file extensive reports later on. Maurice was reconciled, for his own part, to encountering attractive females who were convinced he was too short to be seen with them.

It was Maurice, his eye always alert for a jarring note in the composition of some prospective scene, as he thought of every street or room he encountered, who was first aware of the intrusive note. This time it took the form of a bearded gray goat, which made curious sounds as if to capture his attention further.

"By heavens, I do believe that Maury has found someone at last," young Parfitt chuckled at his side. "Hairy, but willing."

Maurice's eyes, following the gray rope by which the beast was held, widened in pleasure. The girl at the other end was certainly young, perhaps his own age, and deucedly attractive. Dark-haired with small eyes and what looked through the cape like a trim figure indeed, her thrust-out chin reminded him of a subject he had recently painted, but this one's skin was milky-white and therefore almost certainly lovely to the touch.

"She's mine," he said with a quiet confidence that surprised him, having noted that she was hardly taller than he. "I saw her first."

One of his friends sighed in envy that might have been exaggerated and joined the other to walk off and wait at Devonshire House if Maurice found it necessary to meet them once more. Such a later meeting was part of the biweekly routine upon these jaunts of theirs.

"Thank heavens," Parfitt said to Hubert Joyce. "I thought that Maury was going to be the man left out forever, if you know what I mean."

"I should hope not!"

"When we next see him, we must compliment him on his success with pretty women," said Parfitt, who felt himself too tall for a young female of that one's height.

"I suppose so," Hubert Joyce agreed. "She *is* rather attractive."

Maurice, as has been seen, felt much the same about the young female. Although it was normally difficult for him to speak easily upon meeting a young woman, he was able on this occasion to smile down at the goat and refer to the beast.

"Your companion isn't easy to handle."

The girl was silent.

Maurice, flushing at what she might have considered his impertinence, nonetheless continued along the course he had set.

"I don't think we have been introduced," he added, ostensibly addressing himself to the goat. He took off his black hat and bowed. "My name is—"

That was when the girl laughed, and her previous silence was explained almost immediately. *"C'est très drôle, ça,"* she said.

"Oh, a Frenchie!" Maurice looked delighted. "My mother says that she approves of all things French except, perhaps, a recent Corsican ruler of your country who shall be nameless. I can see very well why men would approve also in at least this one restricted case."

Maurice, who always considered himself a hard-eyed realist, felt certain that never had he been more quick in seeing through to the meaning of a situation and speaking that truth accordingly. When a cynic falls in love, as Maurice didn't yet appreciate, he falls with the greatest celerity.

The girl gave a radiant smile, having understood his tone, if not every word.

They walked on together. It developed, in largely one-sided conversation, that Miss Nina Fontaine was parading the goat because a British friend had challenged her to do so. Maurice felt better, somehow, after inferring that much.

Mlle. Fontaine spoke English only with difficulty, and often understood inflections and pauses rather than meanings as such.

"We must see one another often," Maurice said, almost as if it was an order.

His little Venus shrugged lightly, accenting the maiden white of her walking dress and the contrasting turquoise of her cape. It now seemed to Maurice, with his artist's eye, that the girl was dressed perfectly in colors that contrasted without jarring and in garments that fit precisely. It was hardly to the point at this time, but it constituted one more reason for being favorably disposed to this exceptional, this extraordinarily marvelous female.

"I cannot believe that you don't reciprocate my feelings," Maurice insisted. Had he been in a self-depracating mood, he would have promptly considered that the girl's feelings for him had faded.

"There is no much time," Nina Fontaine said.

"We will have to use the time that exists, and then make other arrangements." Maurice felt more determined now, having learned that Nina was visiting from across the infernal Channel for a few days. She and her family were staying in New Burlington Street with friends.

Nina nodded at his resolve to spend more time with her. She didn't disbelieve him, but was inclined to accept facts as they presented themselves.

"On the first day of March, I leave for 'ome," she said. "With my *maman* and papa."

"Just the luck for me to meet someone who will leave in a few days." He reached out a hand to take hers. Nina's touch was warm and firm, returning pressure without stint. "I shall make it a point to visit you in Paris," he said, pronouncing the name of that city in what he confidently imagined was the style of its natives, with a guttural *r* and a long *e*. "I expect I'll have more time than I used to, for a while."

The strong reaction to her that he was feeling could most assuredly be called love. No longer did it surprise him, for example, that only a Frenchwoman would be of the proper height to flatter his own, nor did it occur to him that Nina must have had difficulty with French males constructed as high as the Crystal Palace in Hyde Park.

"Will you be free tomorrow?" he asked.

"Not at all till I leave," she said sadly. "This is the only walk I can take, and only with a friend far be'ind to see that I am indeed escort to this goat. My family are determined to buy everything in the shops, especially my *maman*."

It seemed ludicrous that anyone would come over from Paris to shop in London. Had Nina's parents been in earshot, the normally chauvinistic Maurice would have spoken passionately about the inferiority of British goods.

"And the nights?" he asked. "Not all your nights can be taken. Surely I could call."

"Much of my time is not mine because of a ball gown that is being made for me." Nina made herself clear despite the barrier of language. "And of course I am to attend the ball itself."

Maurice suddenly felt cautious. "A ball? On what night?"

"The night before I leave," Nina said. "On the twenty-eighth of this month."

"At the Fitton place?" He was aware of a sinking feeling that started at the pit of his stomach and plummeted past his boots.

"Fee-ton," Nina agreed.

He was about to say, "Don't reserve a dance for me," the sort of flippant remark that would have amused any knowledgeable maiden or even the sort of girl that Heather didn't happen to know wasn't any longer called a dollymop. Nina wasn't one with whom a man spoke humorously of serious matters.

There was more conversation between them, in the course of which he obtained that address in Paris which she graced with her presence when at home.

"So you have no time to yourself in London any more." He was musing aloud. It was impossible for him to accept that he wouldn't see this girl again for he knew not how long. Determinedly he drew himself up to his full height, such as it was. "Very well, then, my dear. I shall dance with you at the Fitton ball."

She smiled her understanding of the promise. Only when the words were irretrievably out of his mouth did he, like Ambrose, ask himself how the devil he was going to gain admission to that particular festival.

CHAPTER NINETEEN

Alarum and Excursion

It would be wisest to say little about the seething torrent of emotion in three London homes on the next morning. Ambrose Pennymore, who seemed as rigid as a soldier on parade, eventually materialized at his father's establishment and pretended to be of use. Clarissa Fitton absently supervised details of the construction of a magnificent gown to be worn by her on the fateful Saturday night, and only gave closest attention to one of the letters she wrote.

Maurice Shaw, like Ambrose, did his work in a desultory fashion and knew it would have to be done all over again at some time in the future when he was feeling approximately human. Briefly, he had done some additional work on the portrait of the Marquis of Thetford, who seemed disinclined to sit still.

As for Heather, she had caught only a glimpse of Julian proceeding upward to Maurice's attic workroom. On the way out, he paused for a mere moment, as duty called him to the Lords. He had time only to press Heather's hand and whisper that his feelings for her hadn't changed, then he was running to a cab that would take him to the Lords.

Heather received one more note that had been smuggled out of Bennet Street. Clarissa was asking for yet another favor. It seemed that Ambrose had declared his determination to attend the Fitton ball, spurred, no doubt, by love. Clarissa had herself been too distracted to persuade him otherwise. Would Heather undertake to prevent him from damaging the cause to which both were so firmly dedicated?

Convinced that it was a necessary gesture after the havoc she had unwittingly wrought in their lives, Heather made haste to proceed. The largely white day dress and russet cape would be sufficient and unexceptionable wear for the occasion.

Maurice, pacing the lower floor with hands behind his back in a spasm of protracted idleness, looked up muzzily and roused himself to compliment her on the combination of colors she wore.

"Are you off somewhere?" he asked vaguely, his thoughts elsewhere.

"I must visit Ambrose Pennymore." Briefly she clarified her reasons. "Mamma will surely serve as chaperone to the Pennymore home."

"Home? It is the bank where Ambrose can be found." Maurice cogitated briefly. "I am available to do the necessary job of a *cicisbeo*, if only to prevent any additional blundering of yours."

"You are kind, but discourteous," Heather remarked.

A brief word with Mamma was needed before her brother obtained permission for the contemplated journey. A three-color hansom, which he insisted upon hiring, took them to Maiden Lane and the site of the Pennymore Bank.

Ambrose, discovered in listless conversation with a prospective client, soon made his excuses and joined the siblings. The young banker's prominent cheeks seemed to dangle perilously on his face, and the sparkle that must have recently enlivened those wide-apart gray eyes was gone as though it had never appeared.

Heather began promptly. "Ambrose, I am sorry for your troubles, as the Irish say." She could have added that she felt the same about her own difficulties, but it wasn't to the point. She hadn't seen Ambrose since the newspaper feature had erupted, and the change in him was unsettling.

"Let us not talk of it here," Ambrose said, having looked furtively over a shoulder. His eye met that of a worker who was snickering. "I suggest a stroll."

"Certainly." Heather's heart went out to the young man. Before the three of them left, she took a moment to stare coldly at that impudent bank clerk, who looked away in a hurry.

The bracing weather struck the others, but not Ambrose in spite of his having left the premises and not taken outer covering for his indoor clothes. He moved blindly toward Southampton Street, bumping into every hitching post that presented itself.

Heather hated conveying the message that had been assigned to her, but saw no alternative. "I've had a letter from Clarissa and she says that you are plotting to attend the Saturday night ball."

"I must!"

Her duty was made no easier by comprehending exactly how Ambrose felt. Almost certainly Julian would have attempted to invade a function to which she had been invited and not he. Without the least difficulty she could remember Julian's anger on that night when he learned that she had previously given Ambrose half the number of dances at a festive occasion.

"Clarissa wants me to speak to you about the virtues of sweet reason and the unlikelihood of your being able to achieve the objective upon which you appear to have set yourself."

"I must do it," Ambrose said, pausing only to grunt as a hitching post obdurately struck him in the solar plexus. "I swore I would."

Maurice was nodding, which surprised Heather.

Her usually practical brother now said, "I am reminded of stories about knights of old who would perform any feat for fair ladies."

"I see no resemblance in the situations, frankly." She was being put into the position of a guardian for fractious children, and resented it. "There is a risk, as I understand it, of fearful reprisals from Sir Samuel."

"He can do nothing to dissuade me."

"Clarissa informs me that a horsewhip has been mentioned as an instrument of arbitrating the rights and wrongs of this matter."

Ambrose remained undaunted. "What does a horsewhip mean if I have the chance to be with Clarissa, to see Clarissa once more?"

"There is a difference between love and suicide," Heather said, performing her duty while at the same time feeling thrilled by Ambrose's ardor if not his wrongheadedness. She would have expected as much from Julian, of course, but felt that Julian would succeed where Ambrose could only come to a sticky end.

It was Maurice's attitude that continually surprised her on this walk. Whenever Ambrose said something, gloriously misguided though it was, her brother would unleash a nod of complete agreement.

Maurice now addressed the central difficulty. "Do you have any plan, Ambrose, that would make it feasible for you to enter where you haven't been invited and are pointedly not wanted by the host?"

"No plan whatever, I regret to say."

"Then nothing could possibly be gained by pursuing the matter," Heather remarked with what she hoped was finality.

"Quite to the contrary," Maurice interrupted. "It is necessary to discuss how Ambrose *can* gain entry to that carnival, and how I can be there as well."

Heather's jaw dropped. In her surprise she was speechless.

Ambrose, into whose body new life seemed to have entered, suddenly said, "In that case, let us seek the privacy we require."

Still speechless, Heather followed Ambrose and her brother upon various turns from one chill street to another. Fog was drifting away. As ever, it seemed to prevail in the shoddiest-looking streets and avoid those that reflected greater affluence.

The trio soon approached the Pennymore family's four-story domicile close to Garrick Street. At the butler's appearance in the doorway, Ambrose said, "Good afternoon, Gateshead."

Heather saw the butler's sudden disquiet when she and Maurice entered behind the young master of the house, but gave it no further thought. She could only imagine her brother and Ambrose embarking together upon this suicidal folly that was now being contemplated by two instead of one.

They walked through a long cluttered hall into the large sitting room. This proved to be furnished with shoddy royal blue curtains, a rug that looked like threads strung together, and light inexpensive pieces. No doubt the furnishings *chez* Pennymore, which Heather had previously seen, reflected the father's parsimony, as was only to be expected.

But this was a time for reflections on matters of greater urgency, to be followed by much needed clarification.

"I am no longer shocked by the perfidy of the male sex," Heather began, making a blanket denunciation as soon as Gateshead had departed to bring tea for the host and guests. "Certainly I am not surprised after hearing Mother tell of Maud McThrapple's betrayal at home." She meant at Hawick, of course, and Maurice nodded. "But I expected some truthfulness from you."

"I have not lied."

"An omission constitutes an untruth," Heather said, with a magisterial demeanor that seemed forced upon her again and again by these examples of masculine behavior. "There is some reason for your wishing to attend the Fitton fete, if I may call it that, and you have not been forthcoming with information."

Maurice said, "I've met a girl who will be there."

"A girl?" His response was so ordinary that Heather, used to his excesses during these recent years, was startled once more. "Are you so intrigued because this creature would be a striking subject for a painting?"

"Nothing like that," Maurice snapped, temporarily dismissing his life's work as if it had been a mere aberration and again sending Heather's jaw down to a point below her neck.

"You, Maurice—*you* are enamored?"

"She is lovely. As dainty as a flower and small as a pocket watch." Maurice was unaware that he had given a reason for some of this reversal in his attitudes. "The moment I saw her with the goat—"

"I beg your pardon?" Heather asked, and even Ambrose, absorbed in his own dilemma as he had been, took the trouble to seem startled. "Is the girl a milkmaid of some sort, and in London?"

"No, she's not," Maurice said irritably. "Indeed I didn't think that anyone in The City kept a goat, but Nina had been challenged by a friend to escort the beast down—"

"If you say so," Heather conceded temperately, hoping to prevent another burst of oratory from her brother. "My only consideration was that your first meeting with her can have had little in common with the way that Romeo met Juliet, I feel certain."

"Could we proceed?" Maurice asked icily, annoyed by the irrelevant observation. "I hope you now understand why I am determined to manifest myself at the *danse macabre* which Sir Samuel Fitton is paying for."

Two incidents occurred at this time. Gateshead, the butler,

opened the door. He was dexterously carrying a laden tea tray. Through the portal, Heather saw the back of a maid who was dusting vigorously. For a moment she had the illusion that she was back at the home that she and Maurice shared with their mother, and then shrugged it off. Maids could be seen anywhere, even in the residence of a penny pincher like Ambrose's male parent, whose last name seemed hideously appropriate.

"We have to get past the door," Maurice said, ignoring the butler's presence. Absently he raised a china cup and saucer from his lap, along with a spoon and sugar tongs. Heather had already recognized a "Princess" service from Mappin & Webb's on Oxford Street. No doubt it would outlast the head of this family.

"I don't see how you will enter Sir Samuel's home without pistols," she said, playing the devil's advocate one more time. "Appear in the outer door, masked, and call out, 'Stand and deliver!' All will then be granted to you, I feel certain."

Ambrose clucked disapprovingly. It was astonishing that he would express dissenting opinions, even to such an extent. Love had apparently made him infinitesimally more decisive, which was one of the many good things to be said for it.

Maurice spoke reflectively. "When we can get into Sir Samuel's reception area among so many others, he won't dare to make a scene and horrify his guests."

"Perhaps not, but that thought fails to simplify our problem," Ambrose said with unexpected cogency.

"Certainly it does," Maurice snapped. "One of us has only to bribe the Fitton butler to let us through."

"Bribe the butler," Ambrose said, as if it had been suggested that a raiding party be mounted against the gates of paradise.

"Butlers can be suborned without the least difficulty," Maurice insisted. "They are a notably understanding breed. I know that if anyone shouts during the revels at Cremorne Gardens, every male debauchee on the premises stands and says, 'May I be of assistance?' Butlers, to be sure, every last one of them."

Ambrose looked as if he was unable to counter the point. Heather, wondering how Maurice had acquired that particular information, nevertheless exercised tact and held her tongue.

There was a gentle cough from above and slightly to the left of the tea service. Three heads swiveled around to confirm that the interruption had been caused by the Pennymore factotum.

"Please excuse me," said Norman Gateshead, himself flustered, as he had never before ventured to intrude when not ordered. "I do not speak in defense of my colleagues, sir, although I could do so, but only to be of assistance by pointing out that your plan will prove ineffective."

Heather, looking at the rather handsome butler, tried to recall what she had heard that involved him. At the moment she couldn't recall what it might be, nor did she blame herself for not remembering it.

Maurice, of course, was taking up the cudgels for his idea.

"Do you tell me (no personal offense intended, my good man) that a butler lives who will not accept an honorarium?"

"In this case, sir, I fear so." Gateshead shook his head, perhaps surprised to hear himself saying so. "The Fitton butler is named Turnbull and his willingness to be accommodating (if I may use that term, sir) has been a byword among colleagues and inferiors in the length and breadth of London. I do not go so far as to say that Edgar Turnbull was ever the leader of a white slave ring or that he smuggled opium into Limehouse. Even a butler may be said to have his limits. But it has been possible over the years to engage in varied illicit transactions with Turnbull."

"Are you saying that something has turned this man from the path of flexible morality?"

"Edgar Turnbull has solemnly sworn that he will never again commit an action dishonest in thought or deed." Gateshead nodded firmly. "I should add that the Fittons have recently employed a buxom scullery maid, a girl named Gladys—ah, Cannon, I believe. Edgar Turnbull has fallen in love with her, and it is love which has wrought the overwhelming change in him."

"A butler in love with a maid?" Maurice was outraged at the thought of passion thwarting his plans to be with the girl of whom he was enamored. "What next, in heaven's name?"

He didn't see Norman Gateshead flush to the roots of his sparse blond hair.

Ambrose said quietly, "It is unfortunate that the man, Turnbull, could not have remained liberal for a while longer."

"If it offers any consolation, sir, he accomplished quite enough damage in his time."

Heather was aware that the butler had turned to look directly at her, and supposed that in some way the now saintly Turnbull had been instrumental in heaping coals of fire down upon her head as a result of that one particular sketch.

Gateshead waited for dismissal. Ambrose thanked him for the assistance that had been offered and gestured with a hand. The butler left, throwing open the door and allowing Heather yet another glimpse of the back of a maid. Something about the image was once again a source of keen disquiet, and Heather determined to satisfy her curiosity.

Ignoring the males, each of whom was pacing the floor in a fever of concentration, she went to the door and opened it. The maid, who had been turned irresolutely in its direction, whirled around once again. Taken by surprise, however, she had delayed fatally. The familiar features were revealed.

"It is you!" Heather exclaimed.

The point was beyond dispute. It was, in fact, Beryl Olton whom she faced. The former maid at the Shaw home looked back. The usually merry eyes were wide in horror, the rosy cheeks transformed to a papery white. Even the shiny dark hair seemed to have lightened because of her distress.

Heather might have been expected to surge back into the Pennymore sitting room and inform Ambrose that at least one of the architects of their collective doom was employed on the premises. Rather than wreaking vengeance, however, she felt only relief that her curiosity had been soothed at last.

"I thought it was somebody familiar to me out here," she said.

Beryl took the remark as a cue for justifying her course. "Mr. Gates'ead was dear enough to 'ave me taken in—'ow 'e 'andled Mr. Pennymore, I never will know—when I lost the situation with your mum—with Mrs. Shaw. I forgives what 'e done before, and 'e wants to marry me."

Heather was not surprised any longer. One memory that had

returned in the last moments was of Beryl shyly indicating that she was going out with a butler, a Mr. Gates'ead, as she called him. It was another instance of romance flourishing belowstairs. English homes seemed to be clotted by passion, with staff behaving like characters in one of Mr. Balfe's operettas and falling into each other's arms regularly. The only sound to be heard below after night-fall, presumably, was that of various couples exchanging vows of eternal fealty. It was an image entirely different from any that Heather could possibly have imagined.

"Very well," she said finally. "May you be more responsible in your duties from now on."

Beryl looked for a moment as if she wanted to hide her face back of the feather duster she had been employing in pursuit of her vocation.

"Miss, I gives you me word about that."

Heather turned away. From a slight distance she heard the maid whispering: "Thank you very much, Miss 'eather."

Heather reached the sitting room door. It seemed bootless to discuss any longer what was beyond help. The maid would ascribe it only to generosity and not recognize the streak of fair play that was so much a part of Heather.

Once she was in the sitting room again, she almost wished she had remained outside to deal with the maid's fawning and fear. Both men had stood up and begun pacing. They bumped into each other because of the intrusive furniture. It seemed to her that the use of action to stimulate thought must be a typically male habit of mind.

"No remedy has occurred to you," she said, disdaining the form of a question.

Maurice's teeth were gritted stubbornly. An interesting portrait of him in this condition might well have been composed, but not by Maurice himself.

"*I* will, though," Ambrose said, once more surprising Heather by his determination. "Some *modus operandi* will occur to me."

Maurice suggested, "We could decoy the butler elsewhere and put in somebody we would be paying."

"That is a counsel of desperation," Ambrose said, stiffly but sympathetically. "Sir Samuel is sure to put another staff member into that blasted Turnbull's place and there would be no time for us to do what was necessary and subvert him. No, we must above all think of some stratagem that could be fruitful."

" 'We', eh? Only one of us has done any thinking so far, and you're not him."

"It might be possible to postpone the ball by having Sir Samuel's house set afire," Ambrose said, producing a suggestion on demand. "That would give us time to evolve a workable plan."

"We couldn't control the damage that might be done," Maurice pointed out, as if in pain at having enlisted a bedlamite as fellow conspirator.

"Could we possibly—"

"I hae me doots," Maurice snapped, reverting in his agitation to a Scottish mode of speech.

"You haven't even heard my new suggestion," Ambrose began, aggrieved.

A series of deferential knocks sounded on the door. The men exchanged glances. Ambrose, his temper worn thin, said irritably, "Come in."

"Excuse me, sir," said Beryl Olton, entering.

"I should have sported my oak," Ambrose snapped, venturing upon the first amusing comment he had made since Heather had known him. It was too late to point out that Ambrose was no longer a university student who could thereby indicate on his front door that he wanted no interruptions.

Heather, wondering if some trivial household duty had provoked this visitation, was taken aback to see the maid close the sitting room door behind her. It was a liberty that Beryl Olton would never had taken at the Shaw home.

Ambrose widened his eyes. "What is the meaning of this invasion?"

"Mr. Ambrose, I couldn't 'elp 'earing some of what you said while the door was open," Beryl began uncomfortably.

Heather and the other auditor were well aware that it must have been the butler who had actually informed Beryl of the current state in which matters found themselves. No doubt the agonies of Mr.

Maurice Shaw and Mr. Ambrose would soon be substantial fodder for gossip belowstairs. Heather was beginning to feel more wary of the lower classes as time proceeded.

"Sir," said Beryl, swallowing as she looked intently at a point between both men's heads, "I was wondering if I might not be of some service to you."

Heather didn't doubt for a moment that the fair dealing which had passed in Beryl's eyes for generosity was responsible for this offer of aid. In addition, it gave Beryl a chance to perform a favor, of whatever nature, that couldn't easily be forgotten by an employer.

"I will confess," Ambrose said, having halted in midstride, "that I am unable to comprehend how you could be of service in this difficulty."

Heather, on the point of retracting every odious thought that involved conditions belowstairs in any Englishman's castle, raised a hand warningly. It was a clear indication that she could deal more efficiently with a female.

"Please offer your suggestions," she said, keeping her tones crisp.

"Thank you, miss. It seemed to me that if Ed Turnbull is in love, there is someone 'oo 'as a hinfluence over 'is decisions."

"The other maid," Maurice whispered. "No genie ever flowed out of a bottle more opportunely."

A look of mystification passed over Beryl's features, but she seemed to accept it that in some way a compliment to her had been intended.

Ambrose sounded petulant. "I was on the point of making that suggestion myself, but was overruled before I could say a word."

"Of course," Maurice said sarcastically.

Heather gestured at the men to stop the sort of unseemly bickering that they would doubtless have characterized as worthy of senseless females.

"Do you know this girl?" Heather pursued the vital interest. "Gladys, I believe, is her name."

"Gladys Cannon, miss. Yes, we've met since she came to work for Sir Samuel."

"And she would respect your request, you think?"

"Miss, I'd say to her that each gentleman is truly in love, an' I think it would soften 'er. Seeing as she's in such a state 'erself. She would talk to Turnbull and 'e would be glad to oblige."

"I'm sure he would," Maurice said, awed.

"I shall certainly rise and call you blessed," Ambrose agreed, with a fervor that might have caused him to be misunderstood in other circles. "And I shall see to it that you receive a packet from me on a *sub rosa* basis, to be sure."

Beryl sensed that a monetary inducement was being offered for her diligence and accompanying discretion. Heather wasn't the only one who'd had long thoughts about doings in the servants hall.

"Thank you, sir."

"The feat still won't be simple to accomplish," Heather warned needlessly when the gratified maid had left on her mission of mercy. "Both of you will have to confront Sir Samuel as one of the reception committee."

"Quite so." Ambrose nodded. Gingerly he touched his body as if he could already feel the scald of the knight's horsewhip. "But it shall be done."

"By both of us," Maurice agreed firmly.

CHAPTER TWENTY

A Second Plot Is Hatched

Heather arrived home with Maurice and promptly went upstairs to change for supper. She was in a mood blacker than the dress she chose for herself. Not only had she helped subvert the goal assigned by Clarissa, but her brother had fallen a prey to the same romantic fantasy that was plaguing Ambrose. The two men were going to charge battlements, if that was what soldiers did, despite opposition that was intractable. Heather was not given to utilizing such exclamations as "Faugh," or hardly any other sound would have passed her lips during the balance of this night.

Matters were made no easier by supper, which consisted of what Mamma liked to call British food. Very rarely nowadays did the Shaws eat dishes associated with the land from which they hailed. Haggis had been absent from the family diet for two years as had porridge and the scalding pancakes Heather always loved. She would have particularly appreciated some reminder of a secure past. Instead she was regaled with such British delicacies as weak roast beef and sickly looking fish, the whole varied by tasteless vegetables, lukewarm punch, bathwater called soup, and tea that would have burned the top of her tongue if she hadn't been used to it after all these months.

"British food," she said sullenly at one point, "has made more Scots nationalists than any battlefield victories."

Mrs. Shaw looked anxiously at her chick. "Are you ill, Heather?"

"No, Mamma, thank you for inquiring."

"It seems, then, that you want a certain amount of cheering up."

Heather's senses were suddenly regaled by an image of Mrs. Shaw wearing spangled clothes as she rode an elephant. In her current state of mind, Heather was not amused even by that.

Mamma waited until supper was finished to ask Maurice whether or not he had made any plans for the evening. Maurice confessed that he would stay at home and wait for a communication from Mr. Ambrose Pennymore about the reactions of Edgar Turnbull, the butler, to the suicidal fray upon which the two young men were determined to embark.

"In that case," said Mrs. Shaw imperiously, "we will have a family entertainment tonight."

Heather groaned inwardly. No doubt Mamma was determined to offer good cheer.

With a fine disregard for candle holders, mirrors, whatnots, fans, vases, houseplants, and ostrich feathers in the family's large sitting room, this night's entertainment began.

Mrs. Shaw, who fancied herself as a pianist, smiled before rendering some song about all being for the best in the world. Somewhere a dog was involved, judging from the *sprechstimme* in which words were offered, and a cat and—if Heather wasn't mistaken—a flock of birds. The vision of all these animals encouraging each other in song was the stuff of nightmares, but Heather applauded politely with her brother when the ordeal had blessedly been concluded.

Sitting in an armchair, feet planted firmly on the carpeted flooring, sandy brows raised over widened blue eyes, Maurice introduced the song which would represent his contribution to the family night.

"This is a music hall confection which Marie Francis sings." He cleared his throat.

Heather, knowing the reputation of the *artiste* in question, expected from the first to hear a song that would not have won approval from the congress of forward-looking animals which Mamma had invoked.

> "One fine day at Balmoral,
> Whilst resting on a laurel,
> A certain Queen turned to a certain consort
>   before they could possibly quarrel.
> Her tones they were tart,

Her attitude smart,
And with a glance at her nippers she spoke
　　from the heart.
Oh-h-h-h!
Enough is enough,
So many are enough,
One may be right,
Two can be bright,
After three they're a fright,
Enough is enough!
I'm sorry, my dear,
Although I'll be here,
Our relations from this night must be—"

Mamma called out, "Stop it at this moment!"

Maurice looked affronted. "But it's a song about reality and not about foolish animals."

"There are realities," said Mamma, looking at Heather as if she expected her daughter's approval, "which we can do without."

The quarrel that followed did not end until Maurice stormed out of the house, presumably for a flutter at gambling. Heather envied him the freedom of motion, in having been able to leave the women to conclude their evening with card games at home.

"Your brother thinks that he is a single weapon against what he calls hypocrisy," said Mrs. Shaw, still smarting from the recent exchange of bitter words.

"He is convinced of it, Mamma," Heather opined, "to a greater extent than you know."

She made some excuse to retire early, but found sleep difficult to come by. In the middle of the night she woke briefly, then reminded herself that she couldn't indite a letter to Clarissa with any hope of its being passed along by that young lady's father. After which, she realized that a further scandal involving Maurice would be of no aid to accelerating her marriage to Julian.

Consequently, she was lost to any attempt at repose until the recollection struck her that Julian would be paying a visit to the house tomorrow morning so that the painting of his portrait could continue. Not wanting him to see her after a sleepless night, she gritted her teeth and ordered herself to sleep. After a long pause, she did so.

Heather awoke earlier than usual and made a point of washing her face three times (on the well-known principle that the third time is the charm) with Hudson's Soap. Her hair was combed vigorously until the number of red tendrils that departed her scalp became a possible cause for alarm. Despite Mrs. Shaw's oft-repeated warnings that no respectable girl wore scent in the morning, Heather impulsively doused her earlobes and the middle of her chest with Frangipani everlasting perfume.

After applying warm water to her chest on second thought without entirely eliminating the scent, she inserted herself into a lilac silk day dress with black satin checkers. She decided on close inspection that the garment played hob with her sky-blue eyes. For the first time she wondered what devil's-imp had caused her to purchase the monstrosity. Anyone telling her that she looked well inside it would have earned skeptically raised brows as a reward.

Julian arrived at eight-thirty ack emma and held hands briefly with her, then hurried up to the tyrant's lair so that Maurice could take further advantage of what he justly called the best light.

Near morning's end, a petulant Maurice suddenly appeared at the top of the attic stairs. He didn't need to bend over very far as he called to Heather on the second flight.

"His Lordship feels you might want to see the painting, far as it's gone." Maurice himself obviously didn't think too highly of an inspection by a burgeoning critic in his immediate family.

Heather, bunching up the dress gracefully, navigated the stairs. Keeping her head down for the last stage of her progress, she entered the attic room. Julian was at ease, sneezing cheerfully after a pinch of the snuff in which he occasionally indulged. Heather returned his smile, contented at being in the same room with him, misshapen though the room might be.

"Please show it to her," Julian said.

With poor grace, Maurice complied. The portrait, from the waist upward, showed Julian seated alertly. The browns of his pupils and eyes had been caught perfectly, even in the work's uncompleted state. There was a clear indication that the subject had seen much of the outdoors. It was possible to look at it and know that his voice was carefully modulated but strong. Her brother possessed a skill that was not to be gainsaid.

"You don't like it as much as it deserves to be liked," Maurice remarked after a look at his sibling.

"My reservations are minor." Indeed, these were confined to the brushwork around the edges and the untextured appearance that they presented. During a brief but lively discussion blessedly free of acrimony, Maurice made it clear that he intended to polish that aspect of the work.

"Very well," her brother growled as peace was restored. "I will leave the two of you alone here so that you may slang me behind my back. I will add that I also intend for the door to remain open."

His next actions were suited to the words, and she found herself in the *atelier* with the man she had come to love. Julian took her hands, then kissed her. It needed an effort, as ever, to pull away from him. Once more she keenly regretted the necessity of doing so.

"Perhaps we should descend."

"I have to make my departure soon enough," Julian admitted, and there could be no doubting where he was going to find himself. "As it is, I need a few minutes to speak privately with you."

"Oh, to speak," Heather echoed in a small voice. She didn't know whether or not she was pleased by this statement of his goal.

"I have naturally been in conversation with your brother and he has informed me of what he and Mr. Ambrose Pennymore are intending to do on the Saturday night of the Fitton ball."

"And has he told you that I am a reluctant conniver at such underhanded behavior?"

"It was indicated to me," Julian answered reflectively. "I can say that I remain far from surprised to know it."

A compliment was intended, but she felt too edgy to make the slightest acknowledgment. It did seem as if Maurice had enlisted Julian's services to persuade her of the rightness behind his actions. Heather's experience of men, limited in some ways though it was, informed her that one of the breed would always support the excesses of another.

"Do you feel that I must agree to his folly? It is of little import whether or not I do for he will perform whatever action he chooses. I have not yet put it to him that his involvement in another difficulty would hurt your chances and mine of an early union, but it will change nothing if I tell him."

Several expressions she couldn't categorize chased one another across Julian's mobile features.

"I suppose there is some chance of a difficulty along those lines, to be sure." He nodded. "However, it is not what I wish to speak of."

She cocked her head to express curiosity, and certainly some disappointment as well.

His smile was as calming as his next words were unsettling. "In my opinion, my dear, it is important for you to be there, too."

"Me?" She made light of it. "Are you worried that, as a fellow guest yourself, you will be swayed by such nymphs as you are certain to encounter?"

"Not at all," he said with patent sincerity, and shook his head in opposition to a sudden thought to offer the most convincing show of affection as proof that his heart remained engaged. "In my opinion, you are the only one whose presence can cause the plans of others to succeed."

"How can that be?"

"I have had an idea along those lines."

In the fewest possible words, he sketched it for her.

Heather listened with astonishment. Unless Sir Samuel began to foam at the mouth like a rabid dog and demand that all interlopers be ejected before being drawn and quartered, a memorable night would ensue that was likely to change several lives for the better.

Rather than be shocked or burst into laughter, Heather contented herself with a modest look downward.

She finally whispered, "But what could I tell Mamma when I leave the house to go there?"

A pause showed that Julian was perplexed by this dilemma. He suddenly chuckled.

"Ask her to join you," he said. "I cannot believe that Sir Samuel will want to display the seamy underside of his character when confronted by an older woman. Certainly not in front of those who may assist him in his coveted desire for a baronetcy."

That was almost certainly true. How had she ever managed her life without Julian's counsels and thoughtfulness?

Heather made the one remark she could not have anticipated ever crossing her lips as a result of this tangled web.

"I can hardly wait to discover what happens," she said.

They smiled at each other.

CHAPTER TWENTY-ONE

Stinting Hospitality

Every room was lighted in the Bennet Street home of Sir Samuel Fitton and his daughter. A landau brought an imposing older couple to the door. Three daughters, leaving the carriage before them, followed in single file on the way inside. Lady Denby, the former Honoria Waynflete, took advantage of the pause while cloaks were being put away. She whispered to her tolerant husband that the domicile was furnished so sparsely that being inside it made her uneasy.

"Surely the father could afford gimcracks and gewgaws," said Lady Denby. "And do you see the butler himself on this level and making the first announcements?"

"Most unusual," His Lordship agreed, wondering if Sir Samuel had put out a good table.

While Lady Denby issued last-minute warnings to her daughters, Turnbull shouted the family name as Denbigh. The parents and daughters moved up the long stairway with Her Ladyship leading all the rest.

A footman on the first landing repeated the family name as Bligh, perhaps confusing the rigid Denby with the deceased captain of the ill-fated cargo ship *Bounty*. "An understandable error," as Denby told his favorite daughter.

The footman outside the door called out the family name as Trembly. *"That,"* said Lady Denby, "is an understandable error."

Clarissa, greeting guests from the traditional position just inside the doorway, smiled confidently. She had reason to do so. For this occasion she had purchased material for a ball dress of white tulle over white glacé, with a skirt gathered up in festoons by chains of pearl. In the center of the draped corsage was a bouquet of white camellias. The sleeves were formed of a single puff and frill. On each shoulder was an agrafe of pearls. Lady Denby, reminded of the evenings she had known when a maiden, swallowed and looked away. Tears formed in her eyes.

"You are magnificent tonight, my dear," she said upon regaining control of herself. It was necessary to introduce the daughters again, as Clarissa had met them only once and had forgotten their names.

Denby, his own compliments handsomely paid, looked around for Sir Samuel. The knight was taking advantage of the freedom which tradition granted him and was in conversation with a youthful couple. When he looked away, his glance caught sight of Denby. He came forward, hands outstretched.

"My Lord, you honor my home by your presence."

"Thank you," Denby said. Having been schooled by his young colleague the Marquis of Thetford back at the Lords, he suddenly glanced around and feigned disappointment as he turned back to the host.

"I don't see my young friend, Mr. Ambrose Pennymore," said His Lordship. "I can only infer that he has not yet arrived."

Sir Samuel looked as if he had suddenly found himself frozen in a statue of ice. Every part of him that was visible seemed to have been glazed over.

"I bear a message for young Ambrose, and I felt sure I could deliver it here," Denby proceeded. "No doubt he would not give up the chance to admire your beautiful daughter. I feel sure he will be with us presently, and cause the ball to be a noteworthy occasion."

And joining his wife and progeny, he left a baffled knight behind.

By eleven-thirty, many guests were entering. Already some girls waited near the stairs as if to greet any handsome and unattached young male. Every one held a dance card prominently, but the number of dances that were engaged couldn't be determined by an onlooker.

The musicians, hidden behind varied stylish decorations of a denseness that Honoria Denby might have approved, tore into a *valse* as if it had done them an injustice they were determined to redress. Young men were busily "arming" girls back to their parents. More than one hundred eyes were furtively examining the closed double-doors which hid the supper that would shortly be fed to the far-from-ravening guests. The double doors would have been opened earlier, but many difficulties had arisen and not even a nearly apoplectic Sir Samuel was able to supervise their being smoothed out. The knight was discovering that he could hire and fire servants at will, but on an occasion such as this one he had virtually no power to curb their incompetence. Along with many discoveries he had been making since he was granted his knighthood, it could be considered chastening.

He was keeping an eye on the door through which new arrivals entered, after having disposed of outer clothing. Because of his desire to welcome those who might be of help in achieving his social goals, he was second to see Lord and Lady Newlake and their two sons.

Newlake, having paid his courtesies to Clarissa, glanced around and was ready to greet his host. Sir Samuel charged forward with his usual breathy speech about his home being honored by the Newlake presence. Her Ladyship, the former Portia Galton, joined them.

"What is the name of that young man you are hoping to meet here?" asked Lady Newlake, who, like her husband, had also been rigorously instructed by the Marquis of Thetford.

"Ambrose Pennymore, the banker's son and himself a banker," said His Lordship. "A very sound young man."

Unlike Denby, Lord Newlake was courteous enough not to look at the wounded knight. He did hear a sound from Sir Samuel's direction vaguely reminiscent of a cork popping from a bottle of the bubbly.

"Has he arrived yet, Sir Samuel?" asked Lady Newlake.

"No, I—ah, no, I fear not."

"Is it possible that in so lively a group of peers and their families you have simply not been aware of the visit of a mere commoner?"

"No—I mean I would recognize young Pennymore if he appeared."

"Ah, then you do know him." Lady Newlake beamed. "Ambrose

makes an impression on all who meet him. A fine young man. If I had daughters, I would make haste to introduce them and hope for an offer."

It seemed to Newlake that his dear Portia, not content with moderate tortures, was virtually pulling the wings from this particular fly. At his implicit suggestion, they left together.

Sir Samuel, gasping, stayed in place and offered weak smiles to those who passed by. Anyone who tried to involve him in conversation received no satisfaction whatever for the pains.

The knight recovered in part only when the Duke of Blackwell appeared at the door. The Duke was old, deaf, and ridden with gout. His compliments to Clarissa could be heard in the next room where supper was being hastily set out.

At the Duke's side, glancing idly at the young woman, was Claude Yellowlees. Separated from the skates which had been on his feet when Heather ran into him in Hyde Park, he seemed a well-proportioned young man. Clarissa, who had met him only once before and that very quickly, thought him devilish handsome but probably far too independent to listen to a woman's advice, let alone accept it. Nonetheless she smiled warmly at his well-earned praise.

The Duke, who had been coached by Claude, now looked around as if he had the slightest interest in who might be attending this event. Sir Samuel, seeing him, knew with a sinking heart what the Duke was going to say.

"Fitton," called the Duke, almost as if to a servant, "I don't see any sign of Pennymore."

Sir Samuel resumed his imitation of a cork popping from a bottle of champagne.

"Pennymore," said the Duke, knowing the name but not associating a young man with it. "Tight as a tick is Pennymore. Disgusting, if you ask me! I can stand for a good deal in my life and I have, but parsimony is particularly horrid. Horrid, that's what I say!"

Claude, aware that his uncle was making a spectacular error, leaned forward to offer a correction. Unfortunately he had to speak rather quietly.

"Don't whisper, sir," the Duke bellowed, recoiling in spite of that as if from the sort of debt with which the Pennymore Bank had been of aid to him in the past. "Oh! Oh, the *young* man! I hardly know him." With dislike he looked at the often indolent nephew. "A whelp, like so many young 'uns, I'm sure."

At this, Sir Samuel nodded in satisfaction. "Exactly, Your Grace." Clarissa, who couldn't help overhearing, looked upset.

Sir Samuel waited until Claude was leading the uncle over to a chair, then turned to his daughter and smiled.

"There is at least one guest of ours who has no wish to attend a reprobates ball," he said.

Rather than quarrel, Clarissa sniffed, raised her head, and turned to greet the newest arrival with a winning smile.

The varicolored brougham was approaching Bennet Street at a pace that could only be considered overly rapid by one of the men inside the carriage.

"Wouldn't it be possible to slow the horses?" asked Ambrose.

"It doesn't matter," Julian responded. "Sooner or later you will have to chance your fate, so to speak." He cocked his leonine head alertly. "Not that it seems to me that so much depends on the one visitation."

"But it does!" Ambrose felt too tense to groan. "If I am publicly excoriated and thrown out, Clarissa will never be able to justify marrying me."

"Fear not," Julian said, resorting to the mildest of humor. "All may yet be well."

Maurice, who was sitting beside Ambrose, turned to his sister as if to say, "And this Marquis is the man you want to marry!"

Heather, who was delighted to be riding in proximity to Julian, made no remark in the face of her brother's disdain. It offered some consolation to remind herself that Maurice simply didn't know what had been planned by Julian, with her invaluable help. The fewer who knew, she felt, the safer the secret until the proper time. Maurice, in his self-appointed role as social scourge, might make some inappropriate remark beforehand.

As the brougham arrived close to the curb at Bennet Street, a nearby footman was calling out, "Viscount Dimble's carriage stops the way!"

Being well aware of the deficiencies of footmen, Heather asked mildly, "What do you suppose is the real name and rank of that peer who is leaving?"

Mrs. Shaw, who had accompanied Heather and Maurice to offer unnecessary protection to her wee bairns, allowed a rueful smile to cross her lips.

"That might be Mr. Benjamin Disraeli and not a peer at all."

Maurice, who would ordinarily have chuckled at an implied denunciation of privilege and its perquisites, brushed the remark away with a hand.

"We shall soon be tested in the fire," he said. "If Nina wasn't within, I would no more enter Sir Samuel Fitton's demesne than Buckingham Palace."

Heather, a little wearied of her brother's loud disaffection with social customs, said, "Mamma and I will be going up the stairs as you are being booted down them."

"That is most amusing," Maurice responded through clenched teeth. "It puts me in excellent spirits."

Mrs. Shaw said, "Maurice, dear, I see no difficulty in the splendid stratagem which dear Julian has put forward. You need only join us above as he indicated."

Once again, Maurice took umbrage. "And presumably I will not be observed because I am short. My answer to that is no. A resounding no. If the carriage could produce an echo I would shout and the word would come back to you a hundred times."

Julian said quietly, "This is not the place for a family discussion among you."

Heather couldn't help feeling embarrassed by her brother's attitude and a little awe-struck at the same time that Julian wanted to marry into a family with such a quarrelsome member. True, though, Julian had been in Maurice's presence while his portrait was being done and must have become aware of her brother's liabilities and assets as a relative by marriage.

Maurice paused with a hand on the carriage door, then smiled back ruefully.

"I, who am about to meet Sir Samuel Fitton, salute you," he said, and opened the door.

Proudly he gave his name to the scowling butler who was on the downstairs level. Turnbull, for it was he, looked sourly down at the guest and called:

"Viscount Kerry."

Deciding that it would be safest for all concerned if he briefly adopted the proffered *nom de guerre*, Maurice walked up the stairs. Approvingly he noticed the paucity of furnishings, which permitted the shape of the hallway to be more noticeable and give an air of solidity to the whole. Color groupings, as ever, displeased him, as did the occasional painting which had been attached to a wall as if some artist's dedicated labor amounted to nothing more than a decoration. Maurice didn't happen to like the particular paintings, either, and his general feelings were unaffected by critical acumen.

A footman on the stair landing shouted another name for him: Viscount Sherry.

Just before the door the name and title were transmuted to Admiral Percy.

Maurice crossed the threshold. A brief glimpse with eyes experienced in the judging of terrain convinced him that Sir Samuel was engaged elsewhere.

He shook hands with Clarissa, who smiled down slightly. Being acquainted with the portrait painter, as he was the brother of Heather Shaw, she hid surprise and turned slightly so that Maurice would be out of Sir Samuel's immediate sight. Even while reluctantly admitting to himself that his lack of height had made the entry easier for him, he applauded the girl's good sense. Ambrose Pennymore had discovered a treasure for himself, just as Maurice knew he had done, too.

Nonetheless, he eschewed compliments for Clarissa, convinced that she may have looked modishly comely but was overdressed beyond all bounds of sanity. It was best, of course, for a young woman to follow the fashion slavishly, but no man of discrimination and color sense could avoid a shudder at the sight.

"I am not the only invader," he said quietly, offering this agreeable young lady some news that she certainly wanted to hear.

As might have been expected, Clarissa understood without further prompting.

"Ambrose will be here!" Only a girl without previous opportunities for romance in her life would have suddenly been so moved by that prospect at the last moment. "Oh, isn't he a marvelous fool!"

CHAPTER TWENTY-TWO

The Storm Before the Calm

Heather and Mrs. Shaw spent time removing their capes and leaving them in the large room that had been adapted to such a purpose.

"You look marvelous," said Mrs. Shaw heartily.

Glancing at herself in a mirror, Heather was nearly inclined to agree. She wore a lilac *Teba*, so titled in honor of the maiden name of the French Empress. The full skirt was exceedingly plain. There was a high corsage and a round turn-over collar. Heather did tell herself that she disliked the box pleats at the waist and the puff sleeves that she felt had a tendency to make her cheeks almost as prominent as Ambrose Pennymore's. Nonetheless, the effect at the moment and in this scanty light was excellent.

"I particularly like the round collar in that worked muslin," said Mrs. Shaw, repeating a comment she had vouchsafed several times during the last days. "I wish I could effectively wear something like it at my time of life."

Heather turned the discussion back to a consideration of her own feelings. "Is Julian going to like it?"

"If not, he must be a gibbering lunatic," Mamma said confidently. "Go out and make that simple test of his sanity."

She obliged. Julian was giving his *carte d' invitation* to a disgruntled Turnbull and now he said to the butler, "I have come with friends."

Turnbull, looking across at the new arrivals, pursed his lips. A man of sinister aspect at the best of times, he was now almost dyspeptic in his frustration, regretting that he hadn't argued with Gladys when she laid down the law to him about what must be done to help

Mr. Pennymore and Mr. Shaw. Turnbull hadn't known that still others would be arriving without the slightest authorization. He felt that he was paying for many years of transgressions by risking his situation without any prospect for financial enrichment. Love had made a new and edgy man of him.

He announced Julian's name and title correctly.

Julian, turning, suddenly smiled appreciatively at Heather. He saw her rig-out for the first time.

"Lovely."

"Thank you," she murmured, eyes downcast.

Julian spoke now in a different tone of voice. "But it is time to attack Fort Fitton, the last bastion of rectitude in Bulldom. Are you prepared?"

"Yes." Heather suddenly touched herself near the corsage.

Julian took the lead up the stairs, Mrs. Shaw following, Heather and Ambrose in what was called Indian file behind them.

At the landing, instead of Julian's title being garbled as was almost a custom, it was called out correctly. The precision might almost have been accusing, Heather thought. Nor did the discomfort abate for her at the doorway, when Julian's title and name were once more pronounced with perfect and enviable clarity.

She was in the room at last. Odors of scent and drink hardly intruded upon her senses, but the room did buzz with talk and very little could be seen. She hadn't visited Fort Fitton, in Julian's term, often enough to recollect the points of this place when dancers and talkers weren't charging through it.

Julian, being greeted by Clarissa, for once seemed perfectly at ease in London society. The scheme that had been evolved was a shield against difficulties that could turn up. There was a glow in the deep brown eyes, a pleasant drawl in the strong voice. His ruddy complexion, the property of a man comfortable in the outdoors, made him look as if standing between four walls was a distinct novelty for him and it added to his desirability. Heather longed to tell everyone in the room about her feelings for him and that he felt the same.

Clarissa's eyes greeted her. Before a word could be spoken by the friends, Clarissa's features had altered and she began breathing heavily. The sight of Ambrose had not escaped her, as was only to be expected.

Ambrose, in turn, was smiling. He seemed to have forgotten his recent fears. If anything, he resembled someone who had just left the hands of an incompetent taxidermist.

Clarissa couldn't seem to gain control of her breathing apparatus. It was this, despite the other noises in the room, which riveted the attention of Sir Samuel.

The knight hadn't been standing far from the door throughout most of the festivities. True, he had occasionally been ensnared in conversation, but only by peers. The sight of several persons who had not been invited was a source of dismay to him. It hardly occurred to Sir Samuel to wonder how that foul friend of Clarissa's and her infernal mother could possibly have got past the vigilant Turnbull. It did occur to him, however, that these depraved persons must be sent off at once. Fortunately for his equipoise, the knight had not yet seen that Ambrose Pennymore stood on the far side of the Shaw creatures, as he thought of them.

Just as he moved purposefully forward, the Marquis of Thetford coolly interposed himself between Sir Samuel and his prospective quarry.

"I took the liberty," said Julian, "of asking others to join me."

"Your Lordship," said Sir Samuel, and speaking the title this once was like dealing with a bone in the throat, "you took an unwarranted liberty."

"In that case, we will all leave," Julian said. "When I am subsequently asked the reason for my early departure, I will have much to say in response."

"Your Lordship must please himself about that," said Sir Samuel rigidly, pride asserting itself at the thought of his daughter being corrupted by Shaws of any age. "I will not tolerate the presence of these—these creatures in my home."

Julian said, "Perhaps your mind can be changed by the knowledge—"

"My Lord, it will be impossible to change my mind!"

At which point, Mrs. Delphine Shaw suddenly exclaimed, "How dare you!"

"How dare I have monsters of depravity removed from my own home?" Sir Samuel's face was redder than Heather's hair. "Madam, I will not have anyone of sullied reputation under my roof no matter what the auspices."

Mrs. Shaw said, "Oh yes, you will!"

Heather couldn't help turning around. Mamma had drawn herself up to her full height, and the gray tulle of her ball gown shivered with indignation. Even the accompanying dark flounces seemed stiff with her reflected anger.

"You will," said Mrs. Shaw, "because I have recognized you and am prepared to tell everyone in this room, in this house, in all of London, exactly what I know about you!"

"Nonsense, madam! This is arrant nonsense!" Sir Samuel waved both hands, then shook his head and lowered it like a charging bull.

Julian, who had come prepared for difficulties, was bemused by Mrs. Shaw's unexpected eruption. He looked toward Heather for clarification, which she was entirely unable to offer.

"Madam, I have never seen you before in my life."

"But I have seen you!" Mrs. Shaw said, lowering her voice to keep others beyond this rough circle from learning what she was on the point of conveying. "It was in Hawick when you were a young man with those unique exclamatory gestures you were just making a moment ago."

Sir Samuel's voice was perceptibly weaker. "But I have never been to—"

"Hawick in Roxburghshire, yes, and you've visited there," said Mrs. Shaw deliberately, giving Sir Samuel time to realize he had overreached himself. "That was where you met and seduced the dear friend of my childhood, Maud McThrapple."

"Mamma!" Heather was astonished.

Sir Samuel, speaking at the same time, said, "I absolutely deny any of this!"

"Villain! Betrayer of maidens! I have kept in touch with Maud over the years and feel certain that she will gladly testify about what was done to her at your hands."

Heather knew that Mrs. Shaw was tampering with the truth in

this latter revelation and felt that no identification could have been shakier than Mrs. Shaw's. But the knight had fallen guiltily silent.

Julian gave a soundless whistle. "Stalemate, as we call it in chess."

Sir Samuel asked quietly, "What is it that you want?"

"To stay and have my daughter recognized as belonging where good society gathers."

"If you and she will leave my Clarissa to her own devices," the knight said, defeated but prepared to bargain for his daughter's welfare as he conceived it, "I will agree to let you both stay for the ball."

Both Mrs. Shaw and Heather doubted if Clarissa's time could have been engaged by anyone other than Ambrose.

"Very well," said Delphine Shaw, as if she was making a concession. "But you will prove that you accept my daughter's presence by dancing with her. One dance with a man considered to be so utterly respectable should be sufficient to clarify this matter to all."

"I—"

"Is that clear?"

Sir Samuel swallowed air. He paused long enough to wish many curses upon his tormentor's coiffed gray head.

"May I dance with your daughter?" Sir Samuel asked, speaking more slowly than he had done in years.

"You may."

As a consequence of this pointed encouragement, the knight led Heather to the floor. A polka was underway. Heather noted with relief that Sir Samuel passed the true tests of a dancer of the polka, being possessed despite his age of the necessary speed as well as the capacity to go the wrong way, as it was admiringly called in Britain. Otherwise, the dance was certainly the least pleasurable in which Heather ever participated.

Sir Samuel soon "armed" Heather, walking back with her to Mrs. Shaw's habitat. Girls smiled warmly at her for the first time since that infamous drawing had been reproduced in the gossip periodical. Men nodded and smiled. Heather heard no sniggers. She didn't pause to tell herself that the British in society were strange to accept her because of the proximity of a wealthy and prudish knight. What mattered was that her rehabilitation was now assured.

Being Heather, though, she felt that her status was conditional upon that of Ambrose. Like an intemperate docker, Ambrose, too, must be saved. Otherwise, realizing what she had done to damage him, however inadvertently, her own improved status would be forever worthless.

Sir Samuel, walking at her side and grateful that he would soon be out of close contact with the young woman (though she was deuced attractive, he had to concede that much), suddenly heard a prolonged gasp from the throats of half a dozen females.

"What is this?" Already he was anticipating the worst, convinced that nothing helpful was likely to take place on a night that was already so difficult.

He soon had cause to admire his acumen while detesting the proof of it. Ambrose Pennymore was in the room. Further, the blasted young sprig was standing near his daughter. Worst of all, Clarissa had eyes for none but that whelp of a Pennymore.

"I won't have him laying siege to my daughter's affections," Sir Samuel pronounced with greater volume than was socially correct. Suppressing an expletive much favored by Arab camel drivers in dealing with their beasts, the knight rushed forward. "I don't care what happens to me as a result, but I won't have him here!"

And Heather, unable to avoid listening to those poisoned words, felt with a sinking heart that the cause was lost forever.

For Ambrose Pennymore, the last minutes had been difficult indeed. Having scaled the heights to this place where he wanted to be, he now found himself the object of all consideration. There was no girl in the room who didn't look wide-eyed at him, and more than one was smiling. Miss Augusta Satterthwaite, who had pointedly ignored him in the past, suddenly made a gesture with one crooking finger that amounted to beckoning him toward her. It seemed that there was hardly a girl in the place who didn't want to become a better friend to Ambrose Pennymore, now that he was named as a notorious rascal.

Such behavior constituted proof to the bewildered young man that he was powerless to understand the mental processes of what was mockingly called the fair sex. And it gave still more proof, if any should be needed, that Clarissa Fitton was the only girl in the world with whom he could be happy.

About this, at the moment, there appeared to be two schools of thought. The Shaws and Julian Wyse, Marquis of Thetford, supported him. On the other side, however, and bitter in opposition, was his prospective father-in-law.

Sir Samuel, having previously foamed at the mouth and bubbled like a seething volcano in the sort of painting that Maurice Shaw would probably have liked to limn, was now making fists as he moved. Never before had the gentle Ambrose seen such dislike in another human's manner.

Several incidents now took place at the same time.

Clarissa promptly interceded between her father and the man she loved.

Julian, who had been going to accomplish a similar feat, halted close to the disputants.

Sir Samuel gestured with his head in a direction away from this room.

"Leave the floor at once," he said thinly to his daughter.

In vain did an onlooker ask lightly but clearly, "Does he expect her to levitate?"

Sir Samuel snapped, "At once, do you hear?"

It is possible that further unpleasant developments could now have ensued under the eyes of many. Sir Samuel might have put a hand in outrage to his daughter, then turned violently on Ambrose. Such events would have been the talk of society until Queen Victoria's reign was ended.

Ambrose and both Fittons were saved from this fate primarily because the double doors at the far end fortuitously opened to that room in which supper was to be served. Through the portals it was possible to inhale an aroma that blithely conjoined several types of fish and meat, many steaming vegetables, and almost certainly more than one variety of soup.

Very likely the Briton deprived of nourishment too long after the beginning of a ball would probably have turned his or her back on the burning of Rome if refreshments beckoned instead. As it was, the auditors of all ages turned to attack the varieties of food that awaited their onslaught. The immediate participants in this drama were not left entirely alone, but observers were now at a greater distance.

Julian said quietly, "Perhaps I can be of aid."

Sir Samuel didn't turn his head. "You have already done quite enough!"

"I strongly suggest that you and I make our way to another room for a talk. Your daughter and Mr. Pennymore will behave decorously in public."

"I have no intention of obliging you in any way."

Heather spoke, rather than listen to a clash of wills. "Won't you oblige even if he can help gain you the baronetcy you desire?"

Sir Samuel now turned to look first at Heather and then the peer. His face was a study in diverse emotions.

"He—? Well, I am sure there will be no harm done in public," he said after a pause, as if the concept had originated with him. "Clarissa, I have changed my mind. Stay in this room until I come back!"

Without looking behind him, Sir Samuel started to the banquet room. From there, no doubt, another exit would take him to a place where quiet could be anticipated and sustained. Along the way, he passed the artist Maurice Shaw in absorbed conversation with a girl even smaller than Shaw himself. Sir Samuel knew perfectly well that the portraitist hadn't been invited. Rather than make an issue of the matter, he contented himself with a snarl and went on his way.

"Now, my lord, what have you to tell me?"

Heather had followed the men into a large and comfortable room that probably served Sir Samuel as a study. Her interest in furnishings didn't extend to the mogul's lair, certainly not at this particular time.

"Mainly this," said Julian, taking a seat before the mahogany desk without being asked. "To gain further recognition for yourself is difficult, not so much because of the product you manufacture, but because of your tactlessness."

Sir Samuel pursed his lips, remaining silent as he waited to hear what would be offered to help him.

"Not money, Sir Samuel, and not an appearance of rectitude has sufficed to achieve your objective."

The knight colored.

"But if you, single-handed, accomplished a feat which would gain hearty approval in the highest circles of the Empire, Sir Samuel, that would more than suffice."

Heather had turned to help undo her corsage and take out the folded paper she had been carrying between it and her dress. She put this on the floor first, however, while modestly replacing the corsage before she would turn back.

Sir Samuel, who had hardly been aware of her presence, was looking bemused at the sight of her, paper in hand.

Calmly she said, "I must inform you, Sir Samuel, that the idea for this endeavor came from Ambrose Pennymore. He has asked the Marquis and myself to speak for him as his own presentation to aid his future father-in-law might not receive the proper attention."

Sir Samuel permitted even that monologue to pass without comment. He couldn't keep his eyes from the paper.

"Give it to me," he whispered, "whatever it is."

"One more moment, Miss Shaw," said Julian. "What you must now do, Sir Samuel, is bring this to Lord Palmerston or a cabinet minister. You have to inform him that you purchased it from the—ah, creator, and that the person has given her solemn word that never again will she perpetrate anything similar to this."

"Similar to what?" Sir Samuel sounded as if he was being choked. *"Give it to me!"*

Heather obliged. The paper had been folded into quarters. Sir Samuel unfolded it. His eyes grew wider and more round than nature had intended.

"You do see the possibilities now, Fitton, don't you?" Julian asked, his voice rising. "Here is a prospectively hellish scandal that your unselfish efforts have nipped in the bud. For such a service the Crown, even though all details are likely to be kept from Her Majesty, must perforce reward you by what you desire, a baronetcy or perhaps even a Viscountship."

Sir Samuel had not been able to keep himself from gaping at the contents of the paper in his hand, at the caricature of a cherub with only lines for legs, opposite which Heather signed a supposedly scandalous work for the very last time, and the briefest possible connotation of a midriff. The features, however, were unmistakable. Sir Samuel was staring at a wickedly accurate representation of Albert of Saxe-Coburg, Prince Consort to Queen Victoria.

CHAPTER TWENTY-THREE
All Is Well

Sir Samuel slowly folded the drawing and put it into an inner jacket pocket. He said, "Thank you!" in the quietest voice anyone but Clarissa had ever heard from him. Only then, rising to his feet, did he look awe-stricken.

"And Pennymore thought of this? Ambrose Pennymore? How I have been slighting that wonderful lad! I must go back immediately and make amends. If only that marvelous young man will wed Clarissa I need never again worry about my daughter's future."

On these grace notes, Sir Samuel rushed out, leaving his study door opened.

Heather started for the hall. It had occurred to her that Julian might not be best pleased at having the credit for his ingenious stratagem given to a different man. Heather had named Ambrose as the deep thinker involved so as to accelerate his success in gaining Sir Samuel's good opinion after the setback given to that goal by the unfortunate first caricature. Success carried with it the possibility of antagonizing Julian.

"Wait," he said quietly. "Please wait."

Uncertain whether to consent, her eyes collided with the sight of herself in the mirror against the far wall. Aside from being an unspoken comment about Sir Samuel's vanity, it showed an image of great interest.

For the first time she was convinced that nothing whatever was wrong with her appearance on a given occasion. She saw no weakened feature, no jaw too large or eyes too small, no hair too dry or
brows too wet with melting kohl. An attractive young woman faced

her. Possibly, it was being assured and in love that caused her to see more clearly and that gave her the courage to look at Julian at least once more.

"I am certain that Ambrose will not betray his ignorance of reasons for the esteem in which Sir Samuel now holds him," he said, smilingly mentioning a matter which hadn't occurred to Heather in the rush of last-minute inspiration. "Your debt of honor to him is paid in full."

So Julian had indeed understood the reason for her actions and forgiven them. Her worry had been, as she ought to have more than half-suspected, in vain.

"Indeed it is," she agreed. "Once more, I am a full member of society."

"But an unmarried member, which is considered a deficiency," he grinned, stepping closer. "In remedying that, Heather, I hope and believe that I may be of assistance."

Happily, she held out her hands to receive him.

Mrs. Shaw, who had wandered into the hall in hopes of finding some trace of her daughter, chuckled happily at the sight that met her eyes. It was a sound undetected by the lovers.

Her head was held perceptibly higher as she returned to the ballroom.